Mission Control
The Omega Team Series
Book 2

By

Desiree Holt

Mission Control

Mission Control

Krista (Kris) Gauthier and Mason Rowell are like oil and water from the moment they meet. He never expected the team from The Omega Team, the security agency made up of former military, to send a woman to lead the team he hired to fix his problem: find out who is helping smugglers cross his land from the border. Their antagonism is only heightened by the sexual attraction that keeps blazing out of control. Neither of them is happy about the fact they keep falling into bed together and Mason, who values his unattached existence, can't wait for the team to be finished and Kris to be gone. But when the bad guys are identified and caught and Kris is wounded in the process, the thought of losing her nearly destroys him, and makes him take another look at their relationship.

From Desiree

People ask me all the time if I always wanted to be a writer. I don't know if "always" is the word but certainly for all the years I can remember. I was a voracious reads, as were my mother and sister and books held a royal place in our home. The funny thing is I always thought I would write mysteries because that's what we all read. I didn't read my first romance until 2004, when I was sitting with the same three chapters of a mystery on my computer that had been there for three months. But then my eyes were opened and they never closed.

Submitting that first book was scary, but after a lot of rejections you stop being scared and become determined I'm glad I never gave up, because I am having the most fun in my life I have ever had. (Well, maybe not *ever!* LOL!) So here I am, with all these titles under my belt.

Writing a book is a solitary experience but it never comes to the bookshelves, virtual or other, alone. For me it starts my treasured friend and beta reader extraordinaire, Margie Hager, who has the best eagle eye in the world. Thank you, Margie my love, for all the hours you put in to help me bring my stories to life. And for your friendship, which is a highlight of my life.

Thanks to the ladies of Belle Femme authors—Cerise Deland, Brenna Zinn, Dalton Diaz, Regina Carlysle and Samantha Cayto who are my BFFs. Guys, you make me smile on the very worst days.

Then there is my family. Do they read my books? Absolutely not! But they are the best public relations team in the world. From my daughter Amy who tells all her clients about me to my son Steve who makes sure he lets everyone he knows when I have a book released to my younger daughter Suzanne who is my good right hand and my granddaughter Kayla who is my wonderful left hand. Guys, I could not do it without you. If you see me at a convention, Suzanne will not be far from my side.

My cats, of course, keep me company while I write. And you all have seen pictures of Bast at the keyboard with me. She thinks she should get co-author credit!

Thanks to all the people who let me pester them for information, on all the different topics I tackle, from SEALs to Force Recon Marines to Delta Force soldiers to the local sheriff to the people at Beretta and the folks at the San Antonio Stock Show and Rodeo. I'm sure I've forgotten someone and if I have, I am so sorry because the time you continue to give me is very special.

Last but very far from least are all of you, my wonderful readers, who send me such great emails and posts and are so faithful. A special shoutout to Phuong Phen, Fedora Chen, Shirley Long and Patricia Sager who have been with me since my journey started and in frustrating times give me the inspiration to push ahead.

I love you so much. You are my extended family and I send you all many hugs.

There are a lot more stories to come. Please stay tuned.

Desiree

Chapter One

"Thanks for the update. Yeah, I'll be sure they check in when they get here."

Mason Rowell disconnected his call and leaned back in his desk chair. Heaving a sigh, he rubbed his hands over the scruff on his chin. He hadn't bothered to shave that morning. He'd only that minute gotten back from rounding up the strays and leaving two of the hands to repair the cut fencing. This was getting to be a damn fucking habit, and he was sick and tired of it.

"Nothing this whole year has gone right," he muttered. "First that damn woman, then the lost cattle, and now the fucking smugglers."

He had the feeling a cloud had opened up and rained all over his life.

And, yeah, it had all started with that woman. That female. Both of them half-looped in the hotel bar. Each of them searching for something—her for a way to ease back into civilian life after too much time in Afghanistan and Iraq, him to erase the memory of another woman who'd screwed him over. Badly. A woman he'd believed himself completely in love with. It had turned out fidelity wasn't in her vocabulary. He wasn't sure even by this time he'd recovered from the beating his heart and his pride had taken.

Mason had never been one to use a woman like he had, but that one night he'd needed her, with the same intensity she'd needed him. No name. Nothing but that big bed in the dark hotel room, where they'd done everything he'd ever heard and read about and more. They were like two rutting animals in heat.

When he woke up in the morning, she was gone, slipped away as if she'd never been there. And he'd carried a cloak of shame about it ever since then, because that wasn't like him. Wasn't his style. And making it worse? He'd do it again if she showed up in front of him because, even though it was supposed to be just sex, she'd imprinted herself on him. He had to work hard to get her out of his mind.

That hadn't been easy, or even completely successful. Too many nights he'd lain in bed, remembering the feel of her sweet cunt clenched around his cock. The touch of her hands. The taste of her lips and her pussy.

It was all the worse because, after that night, things began to go wrong.

Some cattle went missing, a loss they discovered when they were moving part of the herd. One of the hands came upon the cut in the fence between one pasture section and a desolate area, and another cut on the Rio Grande side. Some of the cattle were drinking at the edge of the narrow stream of water. Sonofabitch. He was lucky they'd been able to find them and get them back. That they hadn't injured themselves wandering around in the landscape with all the cacti and thorny bushes. Hadn't been killed by predators.

But that led to the speculation about who had vandalized the fence.

Stick Montgomery, one of the older hands, was the first to discover the traces of smugglers crossing their ranchland from the border. He and a couple of the hands rode slowly over the entire area and found signs there had been people moving through there, all the way to a gravel road that cut in from the two-lane highway. Although the ground was hard, there were soft places where footsteps faintly showed, plus not everyone had been careful near the thorny shrubs. Little bits of material had gotten caught, something you wouldn't notice unless you were actually looking for it. The fence had been snipped there, too. He'd guessed both people and drugs were being trafficked and cursed a blue streak about it.

Mason had to admit his security where his ranch connected with the border had been less than sterling but as the smuggling across the Southwestern United States—and especially in Texas—increased, he'd spent some bucks to beef it up. Sensors that they moved regularly so no one could map them, night patrols by some of the hands, double rows of barbed-wire fencing.

But somehow they—whoever *they* were—always seemed to be at least one step ahead of him. Four nights ago, two of his hands out checking the fence line and sensors after midnight had been shot and killed. He'd called the sheriff, who took pictures of the scene, removed the bodies to the morgue, and asked a lot of questions. But the man didn't hold out much hope of catching anyone.

"It's one of two things," Sheriff Shaw said. "Poachers shooting foxes for their pelts or coyotes smuggling illegals. Either way, I hate to tell you, there's not a lot we can do."

"But you're the law," Mason insisted.

"And spread pretty thin," the sheriff said in a rueful voice. "There's nothing that points to anyone. Poachers are rodents who scurry away into hidey holes. And if it's coyotes smuggling illegals, the Border Patrol is already overloaded."

"So I'm just supposed to write off the deaths of two of my men?"

Shaw simply shook his head and sighed. "You're supposed to be extra careful and not send people who aren't trained for such dangerous work out to patrol the area. We'll report the crime, but I don't think there's much else we can do."

"This is why these people are never stopped," Mason had shouted at him.

Shaw couldn't disagree with him. But he'd had no answers.

For Mason, that was the last straw. They'd notified the families of the men, arranged for their funerals, and then Mason dug around to find out what his options were. Fuck the sheriff. Fuck the Border Patrol. This was his land and his men, and he didn't intend to let some asshole use it for illegal purposes.

After getting recommendations from other ranchers in the area, he made a call to The Omega

Team, a security agency owned by Grey Holden, a former Delta Force team leader. His partner was a former cop. Athena Madero. They assured him help was on the way. Tough, former military who could get any job done. They couldn't do anything about the woman who haunted him, but at least they could make his ranch safe again.

"They coming?" Stick leaned against the doorjamb.

"They are. Our own mission control situation. A six-man team led by some guy named Chris who was a member of the Nightstalkers and flew missions over in Afghanistan. Plus, all their equipment. They'll run a military-style operation right from here."

"Nightstalkers?" Stick lifted an eyebrow. "I read about them. Those are some real tough guys. They'll take care of this shit."

"Only the pilot is a Nightstalker," Mason corrected him. "But they are all former military. Different branches, though."

"Well, whatever." Stick shook his head. "We need help bad, that's for sure. Where you planning to house them?"

"I told Grey Holden, one of the partners, sleeping quarters wouldn't be a problem. We haven't used the second bunkhouse in some time. It can also serve as their headquarters while they're here."

"Good idea. That would have been my suggestion, too."

Mason pushed himself up from his chair. "They can't get here a minute too soon to suit me." He glanced at his watch. "Which, according to Grey, should be at three thirty, about fifteen minutes from now. The guys finish fixing that last section of fencing?"

"They should be back any minute. Want to give them a heads up on what's going on?"

"I do, so we'd best get to it. Come on. Let's head out to the barn."

Stick had been with the ranch for a lot of years, and Mason relied on him more and more as time passed. The man was smart, savvy, and knew his way around ranch animals. Unfortunately, he wasn't quite as good with people as he was with animals, which was why he would never be foreman. But Mason felt more comfortable with Stick than Greg Ruiz, the man who held that position.

When they reached the yard, he stopped in front of the barn, taking in the scene, inhaling the tantalizing aroma of hay, cattle, horses, and yes, even manure. He'd grown up with it, and nothing smelled better to him. It was the scent of his land, the ranch that had been in his family for three generations.

And now some asshole was using his land as a smugglers' trail and killing his men when they got in the way. Thinking about it made his blood boil. He hoped The Omega Team was as good as advertised.

He had finished giving the men a heads up on the situation when he heard a sound echoing from above, a sharp noise as if something was slapping the air. He squinted at a dark spot in the distant sky that grew larger and larger as it grew closer. In seconds, a sleek helicopter, black with an interlinked MC on the side, hovered over the pasture closest to the barn then slowly descended to the ground. Mason was no expert on helos, but even he knew this was one fucking expensive piece of machinery. Well, he'd been told they didn't come cheap, and the retainer he'd sent was a hell of a lot more than pocket change.

It was more than worth the expense, however. If his ranch became a known passage for people trafficking in illegal aliens, drugs, and who knew what else, the Border Patrol or the Texas Rangers, or maybe both, could come in and shut him down. Not to mention the danger of having such traffic on his land. He felt comfortable knowing everyone on the team was former military. Mason himself had served a tour in Afghanistan four years ago and had confidence he was getting seasoned warriors.

"Better bring the truck out," he told Stick. "They'll have equipment to haul to the bunkhouse."

As the blades slowed their whapping motion, he left Stick to fetch the pickup and jogged out to greet the pilot and passengers. He was anxious to meet this Chris who Grey Holden said was one of his best, not only as a pilot, but also as a team leader. Hell, a Nightstalker pilot was aces in his book. Everyone knew they were the best of the best.

The door of the cabin slid open, and four men dropped easily to the ground. Others still inside began handing out duffel bags and HardBody cases to them. They stacked it all efficiently, duffels to one side, cases to the other, ready for loading into the pickup.

The pilot remained in the cabin, checking the controls, head bent low and face shielded by a baseball cap. For a nanosecond, he thought there was something familiar about the person, but then he gave himself a mental shake. He'd never met any of these people before. None of their names were

13

familiar.

He tried to get a better look at the guy still in the helo and thought he saw a ponytail hanging through the opening in the back of the cap. Great. Was this some long-haired asshole he'd have to deal with? What kind of team leader was that? He couldn't imagine Grey would send a guy whose attitude would get in the way of the operation. Especially as the leader. Well, he guessed it made no never mind to him. He just wanted him to get the job done.

He waited until everything was unloaded and everyone on the ground before stepping forward to introduce himself. He was pleased to see they were all hard, seasoned muscular men with firm handshakes and a no-nonsense look in their eyes.

"We'll want to sit down with you as soon as we haul all this to the bunkhouse," the man named Ted Hollister said. "Our team leader wants to get going on this as soon as possible."

"Can't be soon enough for me," Mason agreed. "The quicker the better."

"We have aerial maps of the ranch," he added, "but we'll take anything else you can give us."

"I have those the appraisal district uses. They're pretty detailed."

"Good." Hollister nodded. "We need to be as specific in locations as possible."

Mason glanced toward the chopper. "I'm anxious to meet your team leader. Chris, right?"

A tiny smile teased at the corners of Ted's mouth. "Yeah. Give it a minute or so."

A faint thread of anxiety wiggled its way through Mason. What was that almost smile about? Was something wrong here? Had The Omega Team played some kind of big joke on him? For what he was paying them, they'd better not.

Finally, the door on the other side of the chopper opened. The pilot leaped down to the ground and came around to greet Mason.

Who nearly had a heart attack.

Holy fucking shit. This was the team leader? Was this a joke of some kind?

Standing in front of him was not the tough leader he'd expected, well-muscled and a hardened veteran of the battles in the sandbox. Instead, he stared at the woman who'd burned up his sheets in that hotel room a year ago. The one who wouldn't stay out of his dreams or his memory. The one he considered his omen of bad luck.

Although her sunglasses partially obscured her

15

face, there was no mistaking the delicate jawline or the body he'd explored every inch of. Lithe and slender, she came nearly to his shoulder. An Omega Team T-shirt fell softly against rounded breasts his hands had cupped and kneaded. Worn jeans clung to nicely curved hips and long, slender legs. High cheekbones highlighted an oval a face and a mouth with full lips—a face he knew he'd never forget and lips he could still taste, even after all this time. Aviator shade hid her eyes, but yeah, that was definitely a ponytail hanging from the back of her cap. Luxurious sable hair that he'd run his fingers through. Hair that had drifted over his belly when she—

Stop it!

Would she remember him? The sunglasses might have obscured any expression on her face, but he didn't miss the way she came to an abrupt halt or the sudden stiffness of her posture. Oh, yeah, she knew who he was and was as shocked. For an endless moment, neither of them spoke.

Mason glanced at the other team members standing to the side, watching him with amusement on their faces. Apparently, this happened with regularity, that the man he'd been expecting was actually a female. They figured that was the cause of the sudden tension. To them, this was a joke, only the men had no way of knowing exactly how much of a joke. He had to fix this. No way could he be around her while the team worked to resolve his situation. Already, his cock was vibrating with the memory of her mouth and hands and the slick, wet heat of her pussy.

This couldn't happen. He'd have to play the misogynist and let them chalk his reaction up to his distaste for women in lead positions.

"Okay," he growled. "Prank time's over. You can head on back to the office, little girl. I want to meet the real team leader."

Hoots of laughter erupted from the men, but apparently the female in front of him didn't think it was any funnier than he did. She yanked off her sunglasses and gave him a view of blue eyes that, at the moment, were as dark as the ocean in the middle of a storm. Eyes that had stared hard into his as the mother of all orgasms gripped them. The muscles around her jaw tightened.

"No joke, Mr. Rowell. And I don't appreciate your comments." She took a step forward and held out her hand. "Krista Gauthier. Everyone calls me

Kris. That's K-R-I-S. Not C-H-R-I-S. And, yes, I'm the leader of this team."

Mason was aware the men were still enjoying the situation. Apparently, this wasn't the first time someone had been caught like he was. But that was the least of his problems. The air between them suddenly filled with tension so thick he was sure it was visible to everyone watching. *Fuck!* On what planet had he ever thought they'd meet again, especially like this?

The rigid line of her posture was a good indication she felt the same way. They faced one another for what seemed an interminable amount of time.

"I don't have any contagious diseases, Rowell." Her tone held a sarcastic bite.

She still had her hand extended. Everyone was watched with evident curiosity, wondering what the hell was going on. He managed to pull himself together and grasp her hand.

The moment they made contact, he realized having her here would be a mistake. *Big* mistake.

Electricity sizzled between them like a downed high-voltage wire. Whatever had drawn them together that night, a year ago, was still there. Mason forced himself not to yank his hand away and took a step back. He hoped nobody noticed the sudden bulge behind his fly. Then Kris dropped her gaze, and the tiniest twitch teased at the corner of her mouth.

"I can assure you," she told him, "I am more than mission qualified." Her voice was even, uninflected.

Yeah, but what kind of mission? With a supreme effort, he forced himself to focus on the business at hand. He couldn't let the message his cock was sending him derail what was important here. After that first little jolt of recognition, she appeared to have herself under control. He needed to do the same.

"Fine." He cleared his throat. "Grey says you can do it, so I'll take him at his word. And, by the way, he wants you to check in with him and let him know you got here."

She turned her attention to the men waiting with their gear. "Rich, text Grey and let him know we didn't get lost."

Shifting her focus to Mason again, she had the same unreadable expression on her face. She studied him for what seemed forever before nodding her head once, as if she'd come to some kind of internal decision. "All right. Let's get all this stuff inside, set

up wherever you're housing us, and have a sit-down
to go over the details of what's needed. The sooner we
get started, the faster we can resolve the situation."

"I'm all for that," he agreed.

"Is there a better place you'd like the chopper to
stay?" Kris asked, a slight edge to her tone. "Or is it
okay to park it here?"

"I'm good with whatever suits you, but feel free
to check around and see if there's a place that might
be better."

"It's important your men understand they have
to stay away from it." With her sunglasses back in
place, it was hard to read her expression. Did she
think his men were idiots? That he was? Or was she
flexing her very delectable muscles to see his
reaction?

Mason tamped down the surge of irritation.
"Trust me. My men won't be anywhere near your
precious chopper. They aren't stupid."

After one more hard glance at him, she hefted a
duffel and strode toward the pickup. In less than ten
minutes, everything was loaded into the truck. Kris
rode in the cab with Mason, Stick, and Ted. Thank
god she chose the backseat in the dual cab. The
others wedged themselves into the truck bed. Five

minutes later, Stick pulled up in front of the bunkhouse and parked.

"I wasn't expecting, uh, mixed company," Mason told Kris. "Sorry, but this is nothing more than a big, open room with beds and some tables and one bathroom. My housekeeper cleaned it up good for the team, but it's not exactly a co-ed facility." He rubbed his jaw, wondering if he was about to put his foot in his mouth. "I can offer you a room up at the main house, if you want."

The look she gave him could have frozen fire. "I bunk where everyone else does. I've been leading this team for a year, and we don't usually have first class accommodations on an assignment. So, thanks, but I'm good."

She turned and headed into the bunkhouse with a purposeful stride. Mason couldn't help noticing the flex of the muscles in her ass as she walked and the straight line of her slim body. It took major effort on his part not to remember her naked and under him.

Damn! What the fuck? He better get his mind out of his pants. Of course, if he hadn't been able to forget her in a year, what made him think he could turn it off now?

Because I'm not some horny kid. And it was just

one night. Forget it. She and her team are going to catch the bad guys for me, so I'd better keep it in my pants. Hopefully, this will be over soon, and she'll be out of my life for good.

He let Stick shepherd everyone inside before he entered the bunkhouse. There was very little conversation. They all seemed to have silent signals as to where they'd sleep and where the stuff would be stowed.

Two of the team members immediately lifted some of the hard-sided cases to one of the wide tables and began opening them. Mason stood to the side, studying the equipment as each piece was taken out. Soon, one end of the table held a variety of weapons. He had no idea what the other equipment was, but figured they'd tell him soon enough.

Kris tossed her duffel onto one of the top bunks then turned her attention to the table. Lifting one of the handguns, she expertly checked it, loaded a clip, and slid it into place then shoved the gun into the back of her jeans. Mason noticed the others doing the same, each selecting whatever weapon he preferred. When the sidearms had been distributed, two of the team members began checking and loading the others, while the rest of the team went back to the nonlethal gear. They seemed to have forgotten he was there.

"Okay, then." Kris stood with her hands on her hips, eyeballing the array of equipment. "I think we're set to sit down and discuss this. Do you have others you need to bring into the meeting?"

"My foreman, Greg Ruiz."

"I'll get him." Stick headed toward the door. "He's in the barn. I saw him when we pulled up in the truck."

Kris nodded. "We have aerial maps but if you have the surveys the county appraisal district uses, those would be a help, also."

"Yeah, I mentioned that to Hollister. Let me run up to the house while Stick gets Greg."

"I guess we're ready," Kris said when Mason returned with the maps and dropped into an empty chair. "Let's get all the intros out of the way first." She looked at Stick and Greg. "I'm the designated team leader as well as the chopper pilot. In case you're wondering about my qualifications, I've been flying choppers since I was sixteen and spent six years in the Army doing the same thing for them. I spent my last year as a Nightstalker, an Army special operations force, flying attack, assault, and recon missions. I flew at high speeds, low altitudes, and on short notice."

"And did a damn good job," one of the men said. "From what Grey told us, anyway, when you came on board. And have more than earned your slot since then"

"Thanks. I've known Grey for a few years, and when I decided to get back to civilian life, he was kind enough to give me a job." She narrowed her eyes, staring hard at Mason as if sending him a direct message. *Don't mention our night together. At all.* "I'm qualified as an expert with both handguns and semi-automatics, as is each member of the team. Okay, let's hear from the rest of you."

They went around the group, each giving his own intro. Mason noted they were a mixture of the various branches of the military, everything from Army Rangers to Marines to Delta Force. They were hardened warriors who had seen more than their share of combat and survived. Now they were using those skills on civilian missions. Not one of them was someone he'd want to tangle with on a dark night or any other kind. Finally, Stick and Greg introduced themselves.

Kris shifted her attention back to Mason. "We've been briefed on your situation, but I'd like to hear it from you. I'm sure Grey didn't miss any details, but I like to get my information direct from the client."

"Fine. Here's the problem."

In concise sentences, he told her about the signs of intrusion he and his men had found onto the land. About the cut wire. About the signs in the landscape of people moving through it. About his two men who were shot at night when they'd tried to patrol the area themselves.

Kris nodded. "According to the border security, the coyotes and drug cartels are partnering and searching for less obvious, more remote spots to cross. Looking at the aerial maps, the Double R appears to be an ideal location for them."

"Yeah." Stick snorted. "Just our luck."

"We're here to make sure it stops. Keep in mind, they may move to another location, but at least we can secure this ranch."

"That's all I'm asking," Mason told her.

"Lane?" Kris shifted her gaze to a lanky redhead who was checking over what appeared to be a padded box of large metal marbles. "Turn on the monitor for those, and let's see if we can light it up."

Lane opened a laptop computer and booted it up, typing in some commands. Then, one by one, he rolled each of the metal objects in his hands as if testing them, watching the laptop and nodding in satisfaction when he was finished.

"We're hot," he told Kris.

"The Border Patrol uses these to track illegals," Kris explained, "but ours are a little more sophisticated. They have a longer range, plus they are moved more easily." She nodded at the redhead. "Lane, you want to explain?"

He nodded. "Once we go over the maps with you, we'll place these strategically from the edge of your property inward. If anyone cuts through an area where we put them, this monitor will light up, and Kris will head out with some of us in the chopper."

"Others will go on horseback," Kris added. She arched a brow at Mason. "Grey said you had a couple of horses we could use."

"I do, but—"

"Two of my men are experienced riders," she assured him. "One is a former mounted cop from New York and the other came from a ranch in Montana."

"Whenever you're ready I'll show you which ones

are available and you can make your selection."

He had an instant vision of Kris on horseback. With him. Seated in front of him in the saddle, her sweet little ass tucked up against his hard shaft, rubbing it as the horse trotted along. And if he didn't quit with those thoughts, he'd be in big trouble. He shifted in his chair, trying to ease the pressure in his jeans.

"Okay." Kris gave him a narrowed-eyed stare again. "Your turn."

Mason unrolled the drawings he was holding. These people were all business, and they couldn't get started a minute too soon for him. He smoothed his hand over one of the maps, pressing down the corners.

"The Double R Ranch covers ten thousand acres and borders with Mexico here." He drew a line with his forefinger. "The Rio Grande is narrow enough to row across in minutes at that point, and certainly you can wade or swim it without a problem." He traced another line. "We spent a fortune installing barbed wire strategically enough to discourage people. We thought. But they just cut it. We fix it, and they move to another section."

"It takes more than fencing to discourage these

people," Kris commented.

He snorted. "Tell me about it. The only really secure area is the quadrant we leased to a company drilling for natural gas. That company keeps a guard posted twenty-four/seven."

Kris bent over the map again. "Show me where the illegals have been through already. And the area where your two hands were killed."

They kept at it for more than an hour, going over details until everyone in the room had memorized what was on both the appraisal maps and the aerial ones.

"All right." Kris looked at each of them. "This is good but we need to see this from the air. Eyeball it ourselves. Get pictures of it so we can come back here and study the best sites to locate the sensors. Mason, I'll need you up in the chopper with us."

"Me?" Shit. Did that sound stupid or what? Of course, him.

"You have a problem with that?" She tilted her sunglasses down and peered at him over the top. "Get airsick or something?"

He shook his head. If she could act as if they'd never met, so could he. "Not me. Let's go."

"Bring those maps with you."

He sensed everyone on the team watching him as he followed Kris out to the chopper. Did his expression give away anything he felt? He hoped not. A former Ranger, he considered himself well-schooled in personal discipline. But, shit! The minute he laid eyes on the woman, every detail of that long-ago night flooded back, and he couldn't wipe any of it away.

Better get hold of yourself, idiot. You have more important business here than satisfying your cock.

Kris walked around the helo to do her preflight check before climbing in. Mason waited until the rest of the team had hauled themselves easily into the cabin of the chopper then boosted himself in after them. He reached to close the door, but one of the men stopped him.

"Leave it," he told Mason. "We need it open for observation."

"I saved the copilot seat for you, Rowell." Kris indicated the seat next to her. "Come on. I've got a set of headphones and a mic for you, too. You'll need to feed me info along the way."

It amazed him she could be all business here, act as if nothing had ever happened between them. He couldn't find any logical reason to object, especially

since it was his ranch they were flying over, and he
had the information she wanted. But, damn! Sitting
this near to her would certainly test his personal
discipline, and she had to know it. Maybe she was
getting revenge, but he wasn't sure for what.

Or maybe she wanted him close to her? Did she
feel that hot something between them the way he
did?

"Don't get too excited," she chided. "I almost
always have the client fly with me. Where better to
get answers to questions."

*Of course. Get your head of out of your ass,
dickwad.*

He had barely buckled himself in and adjusted
the headset when the rotor blades began their whine,
picking up speed, and the helo lifted off the ground.
He had to give it to the woman; she was a damn fine
pilot. He'd flown in choppers before with good pilots,
even some great ones, but almost none who flew as
with such ease, such smoothness and lack of obvious
effort as Kris Gauthier.

He watched her, so relaxed at the controls, but
obviously alert, confident of every movement.
Inhaling a deep breath, his nostrils flared as, over the
smell of leather and metal in the cockpit, he caught a

light, distinctly feminine, floral scent. He shifted slightly in his seat, adjusting his jeans as unobtrusively as possible. If she had this kind of effect on him just by being in close proximity, he was going to have a fucking battle with himself until this mission was completed.

"Rowell."

Her voice sounded through the headphones.

"Yeah. Here. Nice flying job, by the way."

"Thanks. That's part of what I get paid for. How about unrolling the map with the markings on it, so I can orient myself. Doug Richmond's got a video camera in the cabin, and Ted will be taking stills so we can review the area once we get back to the ranch."

Mason smoothed the smaller of the maps across his thighs. Leaning forward slightly, he peered through the cockpit window.

"That's a pretty big spread you have out there," Kris commented.

"Ten thousand acres. But less than half of it is used for ranching."

She glanced briefly at him. "How come? Doesn't that leave a lot of it going to waste?"

"Not all of it is arable. We use the best parts for

raising cattle and growing hay. The part that abuts Eagle Shale is leased for natural gas drilling. The rest of it is just as nature created—flat, rolling terrain with natural grasses, mesquite, thorny shrubs, and cacti."

"And that's the area the smugglers are coming through," she guessed.

"Right. It's only recently, with all the border problems and the immigration boondoggle, that we've had to worry about it. The barbed wire and the landscape itself kept people out before."

"But now someone is using it for that very reason, right? Because they don't think anyone will search for them there."

"Exactly."

The helicopter took a slight dip as they passed over the sections with cattle milling about and the fields with hay waiting to be cut.

"How big is your herd?"

"At the moment, about four thousand."

Again, she slid him a glance. "Pretty big herd, or am I wrong?"

"No, you're right. It's above average. But it's taken us four generations to build it up, and it's a lot of hard work to maintain it."

She was silent for a moment as she lifted them

higher again. "I guess I'm surprised by the scope of it, that's all. It's larger than I expected."

He wanted to ask her if she'd thought he was nothing more than some scrub cowboy with a scrawny herd who was wasting their time, but he bit back the question. Grey had no doubt given them a complete briefing, but he had to admit, seeing it with his own eyes was a little different from hearing about it.

They had left the drilling site behind when Mason touched her arm.

"There." He indicated a spot on the map. "Down there where you can see stands of scrub trees and all those thorny bushes. That's the run up to the border. If you can go low enough, you can even see where some of the ground has been trampled."

She moved the controls with practiced ease, bringing them low enough so her guys could get their still shots and video.

"Do you know how to mark our flight path on that map?" Kris asked.

He wanted to tell her he'd done it enough times during roundup, when they used a helicopter to help drive the cattle, but he held his silence. No sense antagonizing her or acting like an asshole.

Not yet, anyway.

She banked the chopper slightly. "I'm going to take us along the border, one sweep, end to end, then back again. Then I'll fly a little lower so the guys can get better shots of any evidence of people. Be sure you get all of this, guys," she said into her mic.

Mason turned his head to see two of the men seated with their legs hanging over the edge of the floor, capturing everything on video and stills.

He looked back at Kris. "Aren't they afraid they'll fall out?"

Her full lips curved in a smile. "Not with my excellent flying skills." Then she sobered. "Besides, we've done this enough times, they know what to do. Okay, I'm going to fly over the key area a couple more times. Then we'll head back to the ranch."

It was close to six o'clock by the time they landed.

"I'll be a few minutes," she told hm. "Can't just shut the chopper down like a car. I'll do the postflight while the team offloads the equipment. Can you give them a ride back to the bunkhouse and send someone back for me? I don't want to make them wait."

"Sure." He nodded. "It's a quick trip. I let Grey know I'd be feeding you. There's a big dining room in

34

the ranch house where we feed the hands. If you don't mind joining them...?"

"That's not necessary. I'm sure we can find a place to eat if you can lend us a vehicle. We do that sometimes." She sat there as the engine began its cooling cycle, not looking at him.

He closed his fingers over one slender wrist, and she turned to face him. He wished her damn sunglasses didn't hide her eyes.

"In case you didn't notice, the Double R is a long way from anywhere. Shelton's the closest town, and it's thirty minutes away."

"You like your isolation." Her voice had a slight edge to it.

"I get plenty of company here on the ranch. Anyway, we're discussing meal situations. That's it. Grey negotiated it, and I was more than happy to agree. Dinner will be in an hour."

He unbuckled his harness and eased out of the seat, moving toward the cabin so he could get out.

"Mason?" Kris touched his arm.

"Yes?" He paused.

"I...thank you. We appreciate the meals."

He gave a brief nod. "No problem."

He dropped down to the ground to join the

others where Stick waited with the truck. His arm, where she'd touched it, burned and tingled, sending messages to his hungry cock. He had no idea how he was going to get through this whole thing, and today was just the first day.

Chapter Two

They had finished reviewing the video they'd shot and were checking their still shots against it one more time when Kris called a halt for the night.

"I think we've got everything burned into our brains," she told her team. "We'll go out again tomorrow. This time, two of you will be on horseback. Lane, you'll ride in the chopper with your sophisticated laptop. We'll drop some sensors and see what kind of reading you get, checking out the area from the ground at the same time."

Everyone nodded and made noises of agreement.

Kris pulled a hoodie from her duffel, zipped the bag up again, and tossed it up on her bunk.

Lane was at the table where he was back to working at his laptop. "Going somewhere?" he asked when she moved past him.

"Out for some air." She shrugged into the hoodie and tugged up the zipper. "Need to stretch my legs a little."

"Okay. I should have the map set up in here by the time you get back. In the morning, we can discuss where we're going to place the sensors first. And get

37

Jed and Rich some horses, since they're the ones who'll be doing the riding."

"Sure, no problem." She reached to open the door.

"Kris?" Lane called.

"Yeah?"

"Not that it's any of my business, but things seemed a little tense with you and Rowell. Anything I should know about?"

"Nothing at all."

He shrugged. "If you say so."

"I do." She yanked the door open. "I'll be back inside in a little bit."

The October day had been warm, but with the setting of the sun, there was a little chill in the Texas Hill Country air. Kris shoved her hands in her pockets as she walked away from the bunkhouse, taking a deep breath of the night air. The scent of hay, horses, and cattle drifted on the breeze. From the stable, she could hear horses softly nickering and, in the distance, the sound of cattle lowing.

She found a thick ancient oak tree some distance from the buildings and leaned against it, enjoying the freedom of being outside by herself, brain on pause. When she returned to the bunkhouse, Lane would have the sensor placements mapped, and they'd have to visit their action plan for tomorrow. Part of that included checking out the horses Mason Rowell said he'd make available to him.

Mason. Holy shit. He was the last person she'd expected to see here. Or ever again.

That one night they'd spent together had been nothing more than a night out of her life, sort of in an alternate universe. She had been out of the military only two weeks at that time, about to take the job with The Omega Team and hoping to let her hair down after all those months of discipline flying as a Nightstalker and before that as a regular military chopper pilot. She had checked into the hotel in Dallas, planning to get roaring drunk for one night, sleep it off, and contact Grey Holden the next day.

She had, in fact, made a good dent in her sobriety when Mason Rowell walked into the hotel bar. The first thing she thought when she saw him was *hot damn!* At least six foot four of rangy muscle, broad shoulders, and long legs. Blond hair, streaked by the sun and a little shy of needing a cut, topped off a face that could have been the model for a rodeo cowboy.

She sat in a booth, watching him and nursing her

drink, while he hitched himself onto a bar stool and ordered his drink. She was still watching him when he got to the third one, glanced around, spotted her, and eased his way over to her side. As if some unspoken words had been exchanged between them, he slid onto the bench opposite her and gave her a crooked smile.

She still remembered those chocolate-brown eyes framed by sooty lashes, the square jaw and high cheekbones, the barest cleft in his chin. He looked at her, touched her glass with his, and nodded. Things escalated from there.

Even now, there were nights she still remembered the feel of his hands on her body, the touch of his mouth on her skin, the heavy thickness of his cock inside her. They had fucked every possible way and in every possible position. They barely spoke, the only words they used being explicitly erotic.

She was the one who awoke first, seconds after dawn. He was still sleeping soundly, hair mussed, rough stubble on his cheek in a sexy shadow of a beard, the sheet barely draped across the tight muscles of his very fine ass. As carefully as possible, she'd slid out of bed, thrown on her slacks and blouse, stuffed her underwear in her purse, and eased herself out of the room.

For weeks afterwards, whenever she had a few quiet minutes, she'd allowed herself to wonder what would have happened if she'd stayed around until he woke up. Would they have had sex again? You couldn't call what two strangers did making love. Would they have talked about themselves? Gotten to know each other?

But that was useless, foolish mind-wandering on her part. She had in no way been ready to start a relationship, and she'd had the feeling he wasn't either. And now, here they were, thrown together in the unlikeliest of situations. If only her body hadn't reacted to him so instantly. She was sure the soft T-shirt material had done little to disguise the hardening of her nipples. And she had to hope he hadn't caught a scent of her musk because two seconds in his company and her panties were soaked with her liquid as erotic images danced in her brain.

She'd need every bit of her personal discipline to survive this assignment.

Tilting her head up, she stared at the moon, wondering if he was up at the house thinking about her. Remembering. Feeling the same way she did.

Had today kicked those dormant memories alive for him, too?

Crap. She was driving herself crazy.

"I couldn't believe it was you when you climbed out of that chopper today."

His deep, rich voice startled her. He'd moved so silently, she hadn't heard him approach, or maybe she was too lost in her own thoughts to hear him. That scared the crap out of her. What if it happened when they were actually in active mode? Was she letting this man affect the skills she'd honed for so many years?

Damn, damn, damn.

Before she could move, he was right in front of her, arms on either side of her, caging her against the tree. This close, she caught the scent of his aftershave, something earthy that teased at her senses. There was enough moonlight so she could see the strong planes of his face and the heavy shock of his hair. She clenched her fists to keep herself from running her fingers through it.

"Well?" he prompted. "Nothing to say?"

She swallowed. "I...didn't expect the client to be you. If you recall, we never exchanged introductions that night we spent together, so when Grey gave me the assignment the name meant nothing."

"And I didn't expect my hot-shot chopper pilot and team leader to be the woman who burned up the sheets with me a year ago."

"I-I didn't think we'd ever see each other again," she stammered.

"Neither did I. Especially since you ditched me before I even opened my eyes the next morning."

She lowered her gaze for a moment. "I was frightened by the intensity of what we had. I still am, to tell the truth. And I was at a major crossroads in my life. Not more than a couple of weeks out of the service. Starting a new job. I didn't want anything to distract me."

He nipped her chin. "Is that what I was? A distraction?"

She caught her lower lip between her teeth. "I was afraid you were going to be a lot more."

"I thought you were my bad luck charm." He gave a humorless laugh. "Right after that, we started losing cattle and then Stick found the evidence of the smugglers. I thought it was payback."

She frowned. "For what? For having a night of raunchy sex?"

"I used you, Kris. You didn't even know it. That's

why I didn't even want to know your name."

"I don't understand."

"I was in Dallas to get engaged to a woman I'd had a relationship with for two years."

Nausea rumbled up from her stomach. "Then why were you with me? You damn sure didn't seem like your head was somewhere else."

"When I got to her condo, she opened the door wearing only a man's shirt." He paused. "Another man's." He shook his head. "I'll spare you the sordid details, but I was half-blasted by the time I got together with you. I was out to get drunk and forget." He shook his head, his mouth twisted in distaste. "That's what I did with you. And when shit happened after that, I figured it was payback for me being such a jackass."

She touched her lips, remembering those kisses from a year ago. "I did the same. You didn't have a corner on that market."

He tilted his head. "Yeah? What fucked up your life?"

"Stuff." She waved a hand in the air. "I'd spent the previous six years flying choppers for the military, the last of them as a Nightstalker. When you're constantly in a war zone, you lose yourself as a person. And I didn't want to be one of those women who has a string of affairs between battles."

"And?" he prompted.

"And I needed to feel like a woman again. Desired. Feminine. But not with someone I'd have to see the next day. Or any days after that. I needed to get it out of my system and move on to my new job with The Omega Team. So you see? We both carry that burden."

They stared at each other in the half-darkness. The sexual tension shimmering between them was so intense it was nearly visible.

"We can't do this," she told him.

"I agree." But his gazed locked tightly with hers.

"Okay."

"Okay."

But neither of them stepped away.

Kris didn't know who made the first move, but, in seconds, Mason's firm lips were pressed to hers, molding to the shape of her mouth. Without even thinking, she opened, and his tongue swept inside, licking and tasting, drinking from her. He fed from her like a hungry tiger, the kiss so intense she felt it everywhere in her body. Just as the one time they'd been together, he made her pulse thump with an accelerated rhythm and the blood race in her veins. She squeezed her thighs in a useless effort to contain the driving beat in the walls of her pussy, signaling her instant need for him.

She slid her hands up the hard wall of his chest and tangled her fingers in his hair, full and blond like the mane of a lion. As his tongue continued to arouse her, she grasped his hair tighter and held his head to hers.

Only the need to breathe separated them, but when they did, his lips were still so close only a sheet of paper could slide between them. His breath was a soft breeze on her skin, his eyes like hot coals of fire boring into hers.

"I wondered if it would still be the same." His voice was low, gravelly, harsh with need. "If touching you would blister me with your heat and make my cock harder than a steel rod." He pressed his body against hers, the wide shaft pushing against her mound. "It's all I can do not to strip you naked right here and fuck you until neither of us can breathe anymore."

"I—" She swallowed, searching for the right words to say. How could she tell him *Yes!* when they were in this awkward situation?

"I can tell you feel the same way," he growled. "You can't fake that kiss."

"I know," she whispered. She wet her lips. "I didn't want to."

He ran the tip of his tongue along her lower lip, following the path where she'd licked. "I didn't either. I nearly hogtied myself to stop from coming out here tonight."

He slid his hand beneath her hoodie and T-shirt, cupping a breast and pinching the nipple between thumb and forefinger. A shock of electricity zapped straight through her from that hard bud to the center of her cunt. She pushed her hips toward him, and he groaned again at the contact.

"Feel that?" He tilted his head and nipped the lobe of her ear. "I want to be inside you so bad, I hurt. I don't even know what this is but I see you and I'm on fire."

He drew his tongue the length of her neck, swirling it in the soft spot behind her ear. She couldn't stifle the small moan that escaped her mouth.

"This is crazy," she protested.

"Uh-huh." But his tongue continued on its magic path.

"If my guys knew about this, I'd lose my strength as their leader."

He shifted until he was staring directly into her eyes again. "You think they never have sex?"

She bit back a smile. "Of course they do. Just not around me. Besides, there's still the old double standard for men and women. I worked my ass off to get this team leader position, and I don't intend to jeopardize it. Not even for—"

"Not even for the best sex of your life?" His voice was low and deep and rumbled through her.

She lifted her shoulder in a *so what* gesture. "Where could it go, Mason? You live here. I live there. And I don't think you're interested in anything permanent any more than I am."

He was still kneading her breast and tormenting her nipple, heat zipping through her like a trail of fire.

"It can go wherever we want it to. Or it can go no place." He slipped his hand from beneath her shirt and trailed down to her crotch, rubbing the denim fabric of her jeans. "Soaked. I knew they'd be. You're as hot for it as I am."

"This can't happen," she told him again.

"Yeah? We'll see. I'll bet you want it as much as I

do, so we'll find a way."

He crushed his mouth to hers again, thrusting his tongue inside. Before she realized what he was doing, he'd unsnapped her jeans, shoved his hand inside her panties, and run his fingers the length of her slit. Then he yanked his hand back and very deliberately licked each finger separately.

"We'll find a way," he repeated. Then he was gone, as silently as he'd arrived.

Kris leaned against the tree trunk, grateful for its support. Her legs were shaking, and her heart was trip hammering. The pulse in her cunt beat hard enough to reverberate through her body. She had to forcibly restrain herself from ripping off her clothes and screaming at Mason to come back and fuck her. What on earth had she been thinking? Nothing. That was her damn problem. The moment Mason Rowell had touched her, she went up in flames again, her control disintegrating. If she didn't get her shit together, this was going to be a very drawn out, very difficult assignment.

She stood beneath the tree for a several minutes, evening out her breathing and her heart rate. Pulling in the edges of her frayed control, she composed herself enough so her face betrayed nothing and she could have a conversation with her team. She couldn't give them even the slightest hint of what had happened during the last few minutes with their client.

By the time she reached the bunkhouse again, she was pretty sure she was composed. Taking a deep breath, she mounted the three steps to the porch and pushed the door open. Ted, her expert with a long-range rifle, was at the table, cleaning his gun. Lane was fiddling with the laptop, and the others were either studying the maps or working on something else.

"We need to turn in early," she reminded everyone. "I want us out of bed at sunup and on the range."

"If we get a breakfast as good as dinner was tonight, I'm there already," Ted joked.

"Yeah," Lane added. "We'll need to do pushups to keep from carrying too much weight on the chopper,"

"Very funny. Apparently, the client made arrangements with Grey for all our meals. It sure beats having to drive around trying to find a place where the food is edible."

"Did you tell him we might kidnap his

housekeeper?" Ray Donovan asked.

"Ha ha. Let's get done what we need to and turn in. Tomorrow will be an endless day. Breakfast at six thirty with the hands."

"Jesus." Dix Noble blew out a breath and leaned back in his chair. "It's like being back in the Marines."

"Except the pay is better," she reminded him. "And we've had less sleep and earlier start times with other assignments. Man up, you guys. I'll be bright-eyed and ready to go, so I expect the same from the rest of you."

"Lighten up," Ted teased. "You know we're yanking your chain, Kris. Nothing more. We're good to go. You call the shots, and we follow, willingly."

"Better be. You know what happens when you get on my bad side."

Their groans were punctuated by laughter. She knew they would do whatever was needed. They had since this team was formed, and she had faith they'd continue to. It hadn't taken much time at all for her to earn their allegiance and bring them together under her as a cohesive unit. A lot of that was based on shared respect for each other.

She grabbed her duffel and hauled it into the bathroom with her. When she was on assignment with the team like this, and they weren't forced to sleep outside, she wore sweats and a T-shirt to sleep in. Anything sexless. She'd fought hard in a male-dominated military for her place with Special Operations Air Regiment (SOAR), and she carried the same determination into her job with The Omega Team. Which was another damn good reason not to get into anything with Mason Rowell.

If only she could tell her body that.

*****

Mason hadn't meant to slam the back door when he entered the house, but the combination of irritation and sexual frustration was eroding his personal discipline.

"Something got your shorts in a bunch?"

Martina DeRosa, his housekeeper, was setting up the big coffee pot in the kitchen. She raised one eyebrow.

"Sorry. It flew out of my hands."

"Uh-huh." She gave him one of her up and down looks. "The expression on your face says different. Don't tell me it's that female out there."

"I'm not telling you a thing. Anyway, she's got

nothing to do with anything. She's here to do a job. Period."

Martina snorted. "Fine. Whatever you say. But you've got the same expression on your face you had when you came back from Dallas a year ago. And you had it all through dinner. You better hope I'm the only one who noticed you've got a stick up your butt."

"Don't you know mouthy housekeepers get fired?" he snapped.

"You'd be lost without me, and you damn well know it. Mason, it's about time you found yourself a woman and settled down, and I mean it. You don't want to get old alone and miserable like your father did."

Mason snorted. "I think he was alone *because* he was so miserable. Who would have him?"

"Not your mother, that's for sure. She needed to divorce him, but she should have taken you with her."

"Leave it alone," he warned her.

"You're like my own son." She went on as if he hadn't said a word. "I wish your father had hired me well before he did. I might have turned you into a human being. The military took its toll on you, too."

"I tried doing what you suggested once, remember? See how well that turned out?"

"Bad choice." She flapped a dishtowel at him. "I tried to tell you that." She heaved a sigh. "Go fix yourself a drink. It might improve your disposition."

Mason filled a rocks glass from the cupboard with ice and stomped into his den where he took the bottle of Jack Daniel's Black from the cupboard. He'd never been all that much of a drinker, but when he had a taste for whiskey, he favored that smooth Tennessee blend. He poured a small amount over the ice cubes and took a slow sip. It warmed his body as it worked its way through his system, but it didn't help his situation at all.

Martina was probably right, but old habits died hard. It had been difficult enough for him to open himself to a woman that one time. Once bitten twice shy. He should have it tattooed on his forehead.

The smartest thing for him to do—what he should have done right away—was call Grey Holden and inform him he needed another team. Of course, that would have meant explaining why, and he had no plausible excuse. You couldn't tell the head of an agency that you had the hots for his team leader so bad you didn't know if you could keep your cock in your pants.

He'd lectured himself after the meeting, after the

chopper flight, and after dinner to stay in the house. In his den. Behind closed doors. Not to go out there and see if Kris Gauthier might possibly be outside anywhere. But his dick had shouted louder than his brain, so he'd walked quietly down to the bunkhouse. If she'd been inside, he would've let it go, headed back to the house. But, damn, she'd been out there in the moonlight, leaning against that tree, outlined in silver, and looking so hot he'd wanted to strip off her clothes and run his tongue all over her.

If her reaction to him was any indication, she felt the same way. He wanted badly to believe that night in the hotel a year ago was a once-and-done but, apparently, that idea was out the window. And he had no idea what the fuck he was going to do about it.

She was right. They had to keep this—whatever *this* was—under wraps. He couldn't jeopardize her situation with the agency or as team leader. And he didn't need to appear to either his men or hers that he was ready to ignore protocol and fuck any woman who appealed to him. Of course, she wasn't any old woman. Damn it, no, she was not. And, somehow, he had to figure out what to do. Because he knew it would be impossible to keep his hands off her for the time they were here.

*****

Rodrigo "Rigo" Rojas led his group across the narrow, shallow spot on the Rio Grande, cautioning everyone to walk slow and disturb the water as little as possible. Every slosh and swish carried in the soundless night. He stood on the flat bank and watched with an intense stare as each person made it across what, at that point, was little more than a tiny creek. When he had his group together, he checked each one with meticulous care, making sure he hadn't lost anyone.

He'd told Mateo again and again this method of moving the drugs across the border was getting riskier and riskier, but his brother was adamant. With border guards and others on high alert for terrorists, hiding the drugs in merchandise and trucking it over, or even sending it in containers on freight trains, had become almost impossible. Fewer and fewer people were accepting bribes, and danger to the cartels increased.

Despite the fact it reduced the amount that could be smuggled each time, the loss factor was greatly diminished. So what if they lost one or two people?

The others would make it safely.

Finding this new route had taken some time. An offshoot of the Sinaloa Cartel, they'd set their headquarters in the state of Coahuila and chosen to remain small but successful. Because of their size, for the most part they flew under the radar. Using as mules the people who paid to be taken across the border illegally, they had set up selling points on the other side and were doing a nice little business.

The Double R Ranch appeared to be the perfect place, if they stayed away from the drilling area. Vast acres of scrub and thorny bushes and trees assured them no cattle would be grazing there and, thus, no wranglers on horseback to stumble over them. Clip the wire, get everyone through, retwist the wire, take them out where a dirt path bordered the unused acreage, and it was done. A large van would pick them up and transport everyone to the hand-off spot for the drugs. Rigo got paid, and the people in his group could disperse into the area. How they fared wasn't his problem anymore.

A sweet little setup, until the night he'd made a mistake and led the group to what he thought was empty space, only to discover, after cutting the interior fence, he'd blundered into a pasture where cattle were milling and sleeping. Some of the cattle had wandered into the scrub area before he could shoo them back and fix the cut wire. The suspicious ranch owner had sent two of his hands the next night to check the area. There hadn't been enough time to get everyone back to the other side, so there was nothing for it but to kill the men. Hopefully, the ranch owner would chalk it up to an attempt at rustling.

Mateo had told him to find another route, another path for his journey, one that didn't have the possibility of trouble. But this one was so perfect for his needs. There was a place on the Mexican side isolated enough that no one caught sight of each of his groups as they gathered. At least for the time, the Border Patrol seemed to leave this area alone. The ranch they made their way through had enough desolate, isolated areas leading to an exit that they could move undetected. There had been no repercussions following the killing of the two wranglers, so he assumed the owner was smart enough to stay away from that area.

He was, however, much more careful where he led his group, remembering, among other things, to check that the wire had been reconnected properly.

He also began to allow more time between trips. Even tonight, he wasn't sure he should be doing this, but his distributor in Texas was both adamant and impatient. He had dealers waiting for merchandise. If Rigo didn't deliver, he'd find someone else.

When everyone had gathered close to him, he slipped on his padded gloves, snipped the barbed wire, and held the stands apart for them to slip through.

"*Silencio!*" he cautioned in a whisper, touching a finger to his lips.

Ten frightened people nodded. They waited while he repaired the fence then followed him to the dirt road. Tonight, he held a compass in his hand, a little something he'd added after the disaster. No mistaking the direction, this time.

He padded silently in front of his little group, noiseless as a wolf. That was how he thought of himself. *El Lobo.* More dangerous and smarter than the coyote, the common name for people who did what he did. And much more dangerous, as he kept telling Mateo. The wolf was stealthier, more intelligent, harder to track or trace. Rigo would do his job and prove to his arrogant older brother that he could handle more responsibility. And receive more honor for it.

Using hand signals and continuing to motion for silence, he led his terrified group single file across the wild landscape until they reached the narrow dirt road apparently forgotten by the rancher. Then he would lead them through the dense stands of trees to where, hopefully, his contact was waiting. Tonight, he had a large delivery for the man, packed in latex gloves taped to the bodies of the people in this group.

This would be a big payday, big enough to put a large smile on his face as he urged everyone on.

Only one thing worried him. Mateo wanted him to do another delivery in a few days, and Rigo preferred to space them out. But he might not have a choice. If he could not delay, he'd have to be extra careful.

Chapter Three

Mason finished the last bite of toast and ran his gaze over Kris. She was dressed again in a The Omega Team T-shirt and worn jeans, her hair pulled back in a ponytail. Only the ball cap from yesterday was missing. Did she remember what happened last night? The electricity that shocked the air around them? The heat that scorched them with that kiss was so erotic, he was hard for hours afterwards. He was stunned at the intense attraction between them, stronger than he'd ever felt for another woman, even his so-called almost-fiancée.

He shifted in his chair, adjusting his jeans, and cleared his throat. "So what's the plan for today?"

She took a last swallow of her coffee. "Are you good to go up in the chopper with me again today?"

Mason finished his own coffee and set down his mug. "Another flyover? What are you going over today? I thought we saw pretty much everything yesterday."

"I want to get a better feel for the area, plus follow the Rio Grande for a ways and see what other land touches it. The Double R is pretty damn big, but

I wonder if there are other parcels the coyotes might have chosen. Why they picked yours. We flew a pretty narrow path yesterday, by design. Today I want a bigger picture."

"No problem. As a matter of fact, I'd like to see that myself. Because we happen to be the biggest doesn't mean we're the safest or most adaptable for the routes the coyotes use."

"I think you'll see that, unfortunately, we are," Greg Ruiz put in. "We all discussed it when we first found the cuts in the barbed wire. We have so many desolate acres between our pastures and the river, much more than our neighbors on either side."

Stick eyed Mason then Greg. "Maybe that's the key here. We've written those acres off and never bother to check them out. I can't remember the last time any of us even took a ride through them until we went hunting for those cattle."

"And that could be a big part of our problem," Stick pointed out. "The whole state of Coahuila could have marched through there without us knowing it."

"Okay, okay." Mason leaned forward. "Whatever the reason, whatever our excuse, at the moment we're faced with this problem and we need to fix it. I don't want any more deaths on my head." He nodded at

Kris. "Whatever you need, you only need to ask."

For one blistering second, their gazes locked. Her blue eyes darkened to navy, and he swore the pulse at the base of her throat fluttered. His own heart rate stuttered from nothing more than that brief connection. Then he gave himself a mental shake, remembering where they were, aware that others were watching.

"We reviewed the video and still shots last night and marked specific areas on the maps where we think the sensors should go." She nodded at Lane, who pulled the rolled-up maps from the canvas bag hanging on the back of his chair. "Mason, can you make copies for us so both groups have them?"

"Sure. I may have to do the larger ones in sections."

"No problem. And thanks."

Kris was sipping on a refill of coffee when he brought everything back into the dining room.

"Thanks for this." She set her mug down and distributed the maps. "I'd like to check on those horses we discussed. Could you spare one of your guys to guide my men? I want them to ride out to that area while we fly over it."

"Absolutely." He gestured to Greg and Stick.

"One of you has to stay. We're culling calves again today, right?"

Greg nodded. "I'll stay." He glanced at Stick. "That okay with you?"

Stick gave him a slow grin. "Hell, yeah. You can ride herd on your cowboys and their cows today, while I go on a pleasure ride."

"It's far from pleasure, Mr. Montgomery. You'll be out there quite a while, checking spots for the sensors with my guys."

"Begging your pardon, ma'am. I meant it would be a pleasure not to see all those ugly faces for a day."

Greg laughed, and even Kris had to smile at Stick's exaggerated cowboy charm.

"Fine. Then I'm glad we could give you some relief." She pushed back from the table. "We need to get moving. Ted, you and Ray get the horse detail. Let's hit the stables then we can all gear up."

Watching Kris walk ahead of him across the yard to the barn was an exercise in discipline for Mason. The sway of her hips, the flex of the muscles in her ass as her slim legs ate up the distance. He wanted those legs wrapped around his waist while his cock was deep inside her and—

Stop it, asshole. Stick to business.

By digging for the discipline he'd learned during his own years in the military, he managed to get his body under control and focus on the business at hand. He'd do well to keep paying attention, too. This was serious business, something that could put the ranch in real jeopardy. He was paying big dollars to get the best people to handle it for him, so he needed to keep sex off his brainwaves.

Off to the side, where the big corral was, he could hear the bawling of calves as they were prodded into the branding chute and the sounds of the hands moving them along. As soon as they were marked, they were herded into the near pasture where they'd stay for a couple of weeks.

The men glanced over at the activity.

"Hard work," Lane commented.

"Dirty work," Mason agreed. "But necessary. And we do it as humanely as possible, but it's important to get your brand on your herd or it can disappear like smoke."

"Don't tell me you still have rustlers," Ray joked.

"Yeah, only today they have modern equipment and monster trucks. The guys will be finished with the work before the end of the day. Let's get the horses picked out and get going here.""

Kris stood beside him, hefting a gear bag, while Stick took care of the horses for Ted and Ray. When all three animals were saddled and the men mounted, Kris reached into her gear bag.

"Radios for everyone." She handed them around. Same frequency we always use. My headset and Mason's will be set to the same channel, so we can all talk to each other." She gave Stick an intense look. "Don't lose them out there."

He swallowed a grin. "Haven't lost anyone yet, ma'am. Not planning to start now."

Her brow creased in a small frown then she nodded. "Okay. Come on, Mason."

She had him in the copilot's seat again, with the maps unrolled on his lap. Lane and the other members of the team were stashed back in the cabin of the helo with a variety of equipment. In what seemed like seconds, they had lifted off and were in the air, sliding smoothly over the rolling pastures of the Double R. He watched the activity below him through the windshield.

His wranglers were busy culling the calves from their mothers and moving them toward the fenced area closest to the barns. This afternoon they'd start the laborious and unpleasant process of branding them. Everyone's attention would be focused on that, the branding and then tending to the cattle at night. A good opportunity for the coyote to bring another group through. Good thing The Omega Team had arrived when it did.

While they waited for the men on horseback to reach the area in question, Kris flew over the ranches on either side of the Double R.

"Not as big as yours," she commented.

"The Double R has been around for generations. My neighbors were Johnny-come-latelies. Not as much land available."

"So not as appealing to the cartels and coyotes." She banked the chopper and headed back the way they'd come. "Plus, the Rio Grande is so narrow where it borders your place. I see you have barbed wire all along the border. That must have cost a fat penny."

"No shit. But we wanted to prevent exactly what I think is happening."

"Why do you have the empty areas fenced in parcels?" she asked.

"We get wild boar, javelinas, coyotes, all kinds of animals, and this way we can keep them away from the cattle."

She maneuvered the controls, and the chopper lifted to a higher altitude. "Let's flirt a little with Mexican airspace, shall we?"

"Kris—"

"It's okay." She gave a short laugh. "This isn't my first rodeo. I can do a fast in and out. Besides, I doubt they're monitoring this area."

"But they might be. What are you looking for, anyway?"

These assholes have to have a place on their side of the river where they collect the people and load them up with the drugs."

"Tape them to their bodies, you mean." He'd seen enough about it on television. "Even the kids?"

"Everyone carries."

The thought of it made Mason sick to his stomach. "That chaps my ass. I can't— Wait!" He pointed through the windshield again. "There. See? It's barely a road snaking in from the highway. As long as we're in enemy territory, can you go a little lower so we can check for a pickup point?"

"We can do whatever you want."

Mason started to make a comment about exactly what he wanted to do but kept his mouth shut.

"Hey, Kris." Lane's voice came through the

headsets. "You forget where the border is?"

"Taking a quick detour. Nothing more." She tapped Mason's arm. "Scan the area as quickly as you can because I'm turning back." She touched her mic. "Guys, let's get pictures of what's below for us to study later."

"Got it," Lane said.

"That's the spot." Mason touched her hand and nodded. "See that turnoff right there? They must transport them to that spot, unload them, and walk them down that dirt track to the river and across."

"We'll review the photos tonight, and the video. Meanwhile, let's get our asses out of Mexico."

"Hey, Kris?" Ted's voice crackled in their ears. "I'm ready to start placing the sensors."

"We'll hover over you."

"I'm ready to check them," Lane chimed in.

Kris made another slow bank with the chopper then hovered over the three men below. Mason noted that Ted and Roy had dismounted and were leading their horses in a zigzag path, picking their way carefully through the scrub. They were several yards apart, and at various points, would lean down to place something beneath a thorny bush or scrub grass.

"Doesn't someone actually have to step on the sensor to set it off?" Mason asked.

"Not with these. They send out a signal, so many feet to either side. If someone trips that signal, the pod will light up on Lane's computer."

"They're using the track we marked where the wire had been cut before?"

"Uh-huh. Ted and Roy will ride along the fence line when they're finished, making sure there isn't another spot they've used, but this tracks directly back to the path on the other side. For the moment, we'll assume it's their usual trail." She made a slight turn with the helo and slipped sideways. "What's that dirt path over there to our left?"

"Where?" He leaned forward slightly in his seat, peering through the windshield. Sure enough, there was a road—no, little more than a wide trail—snaking through the scrub way to the right."

"None of us ever go into that general area. It's fenced off from the usable land. What I'm guessing is if the wrong fencing hadn't been cut one time, leaving it open for the cattle to wander though, we might not have ventured in here for months. No reason to."

Kris angled the chopper more to the right to give him a better view of what was beneath them.

"There's your exit," she told him. "That dirt road leads out to the highway. My guess is the coyote has someone waiting there for him where he dumps the people and the drugs."

"Yeah. I've got it on the maps, and we can match the spots with the photography when we get back. How are they doing below us?"

Before she could answer, they heard Ted's voice. "We've got them all placed. Lane, you got us?"

"High, wide, and handsome," Lane answered. "Everyone is a go."

"Let's head back then," Kris told them. "We need to check out what we've got."

"You think they'll take a group through tonight?" Mason asked.

"Hard to say, but we want to be ready for them." She banked the chopper and headed back to the ranch. "We don't know how often whoever this is comes through here. Be prepared. We could be waiting a few nights."

"As long as we can get eyes on them and stop them, that's all I care about."

"That's what you're paying us for," Kris assured. "That's why we're here."

"Then let's get back and make plans."

*****

Riding with Mason sitting so close to her in the cockpit had been an exercise in discipline for Kris. His earthy scent kept drifting across her nostrils, overriding every other smell. How was it that sitting next to him, even as she concentrated on flying the helo, sent her pulse skittering, made her nipples harden and pucker, and her juices dampen the crotch of her panties. She'd met a lot of men in her life, both before and during the military, and no one—not a single one—triggered the combustible response Mason Rowell did.

Seeing him again brought back all the memories of that one sensuous, totally erotic, down-and-dirty-sex night they'd spent together. She thought she'd buried it deep in her mind but, apparently, it was hovering near the surface, waiting to break free. Somehow, she had to make sure she wasn't alone with him until this assignment was finished.

She was glad she had the chopper to focus on as they flew back to the ranch. And that she could hang in there doing her post-flight checks after he climbed out. But her team was waiting for a debriefing. No way could she avoid it. When they got to the bunkhouse, she'd make damn sure she and Mason were at opposite ends of the table.

"Hey, Kris."

Lane's shout caught her attention, and she waved to him. Glancing out, she saw the riders had left, obviously to take the horses back to the barn, but the rest of the team was waiting for her. She took off her headset, set aside her clipboard, and climbed out of the cockpit.

"Sorry. Doing my post-flight shutdown."

"What's up first?" Lane asked. "Food or meeting? Roy and Ted took the horses back and said they'd meet us in the yard."

"Let's do our debriefing before lunch," she suggested. "We had a huge breakfast, and it's only noon." She looked at Mason. "Does that work for you and your housekeeper?"

"No sweat. Martina's prepared to be flexible. Let me text her and let her know."

"Good. Lane? Let's haul this gear back to the bunkhouse. We'll grab Ted and Roy on the way and see what we've got."

She jogged ahead of everyone, needing to put some space between herself and Mason. She didn't want to admit it, but being near him frazzled her brain. Damn! She was a seasoned military veteran and an experienced team leader here. Surely, she could control herself for a few days. It wasn't as if they even had any future together. That wasn't even up for discussion.

Back at the bunkhouse, she made sure she was as far away from him as she could get. Lane opened his laptop, and everyone took out their maps and notes. Time for business. She could get through this. She just needed to concentrate.

*****

Before lunch, she approached Stick with a request.

"All right if I borrow one of the horses to ride? I know what I'm doing," she added quickly when she saw the look of skepticism on his face. "I can ride as well as my men, I promise you." And she desperately needed something mindless to clear out her brain. Something to relieve the tension gripping her body that was as much Mason as the job.

He shrugged. "All right with me, if the boss signs off on it."

She tried to catch Mason alone, but as soon as they finished eating, he retreated to his den and closed the door. A sure sign he didn't want company. Restless, she wandered out into the yard, seeking an alternative to being shut up in the bunkhouse with her team.

The hands were hard at it, moving the calves they'd separated from their mothers into larger of the two corrals. According to Mason, tomorrow they'd begin the branding process. Enjoying the pastoral scene, she leaned her arms on the top rail of the corral to watch the scene. The bawling of the animals and the shouting of the men was a familiar song that took her back to her childhood, growing up in Wyoming and visiting the ranches of her friends. She inhaled deeply, the tang of horseflesh and hay a subtle, intoxicating mixture.

"Watching the cattle? I wouldn't think branding was one of your forms of entertainment."

Kris jumped when Mason's voice sounded right next to her. She hadn't been aware of him coming up beside her, the sound of his approach camouflaged by the noise of the branding. His slightly mocking tone of voice irritated the hell out of her.

"Excuse me?"

He nodded toward the site of the branding. "I wondered if you were suddenly fascinated by all this."

"Oh, um, sure. It's pretty interesting." Could she have sounded any dumber?

He lifted one eyebrow. "If you say so."

"I thought I'd take a break from the bunkhouse. That's all. I think Ray and Ted spoke to Stick about riding out this afternoon to double check the sensors. Lane will follow them on the computer program."

"He mentioned it. I told him to give all of you whatever you need."

"Appreciate it."

"I want this thing taken care of yesterday, before we have another tragedy."

He leaned his arms on the top rail of the corral. His sleeves rolled up to exposed a rich expanse of tanned skin. Kris barely resisted reaching out to touch him, feel the play of hard muscle beneath the surface, the tickle of the fine, dark hair. She knew his legs had the same dusting and remembered the soft scrape of it against her skin. At once she was hot and wet, her breath lodged in her throat, her heartbeat stuttering.

"I was impressed at the briefing session. You guys really know your shit." He gave a soft chuckle.

"Although I didn't expect anything less."

His words startled her.

"Thanks. I have a good team with me."

"Nice to be reminded the people I hire are experts."

"We aim to please." She shivered slightly, an electric reaction to his nearness.

"Got everything in place for tonight?"

"We are prepared, although there might not be anything happening," she reminded him. "We have to play this one night at a time. You know the schedule for this stuff is unpredictable, mostly because there is no schedule."

"Understood. I've done some research myself, and I know they try to evade detection by varying when they cross. They try to fool the authorities or anyone else patrolling the area by being unpredictable."

"Absolutely." She had an itch to touch the hard muscles of his arms so she shoved her hands in the front pockets of her jeans.

They stood for a moment in silence. She wondered if he was as rocked by the sexual tension between them as she was.

I should walk away. Go back to the bunkhouse.

I'm going to get in trouble if I stay here.

Mason cleared his throat. "Stick mentioned you asked if you could ride one of the horses."

"Is that okay? I used to ride a lot before I went into the military. Where I grew up. I'm sure I still remember how."

He frowned. "Where you grew up? I don't think we ever talked about our backgrounds."

Kris couldn't help the giggle that escaped. "I don't think we ever got around to talking about anything."

He smiled. "No, we sure didn't. Maybe we should correct that."

"To what end? I'll be gone as soon as this gig is over."

He was silent for a heartbeat, then two, leaning against the corral fence again. "Yeah. True."

"Wyoming."

"What?"

"I grew up in Wyoming. I had friends with horses."

More silence.

Kris blew out a breath. "I think I'll go back to the bunkhouse."

"Fine with me if you want to borrow a horse. In

fact, I think I'll go with you. Show you some of the sights on the ranch."

Uh-oh. She frowned. "Mason, that's not necessary. You can trust me—"

"Afraid to be alone with me?" His mouth curved in a slow, predatory smile.

The answer was yes. Immediately, every pulse in her body ramped up. Leaving the ranch with him was like stepping into a danger zone. The smart thing would be to say no. Every minute she spent with him sent signals to her body she wanted to shut down. The man was like a drug to her, a habit she couldn't kick.

He was a hostile, sexually aggressive male, the kind of man she always avoided. Always.

Tell him no. Right this minute. Do it.

But the words that came out of her mouth seemed to come from someone else. "Of course not. Sure. That sounds great."

Had she really said that?

I'm crazy. That's what I am. Crazy.

He almost, but not quite, concealed the surprise on his face. Then he reached out and took her hand, as if he was staking some kind of claim. Or sending a message.

"Let's get saddled up."

The heat from the contact of their hands sizzled up her arm and through her body. From the way his fingers tightened reflexively, she was sure Mason felt the same thing. Her first tendency was to yank her hand away. The effect this man had on her was scrambling her brain and distracting her. She never, ever let men affect her this way. She needed to get a damn grip on herself.

But he seemed equally as determined not to give her space. He held onto her hand, fingers linked through hers, until they were in the barn and standing in front of one of the stalls. A pinto shifted in its stall and hung its head over the door, nosing at Mason's chest.

"This is Sassy. She'll give you a smooth ride."

Kris stroked the mare's forehead. "Who normally rides her?"

"One of the older hands. He's been using her for ages." Mason chuckled. "They're almost like a couple."

"Won't he mind if I ride her?"

"Uh-uh. Lately, he's been riding one of the horses we bought last month. He'll be glad she's getting some exercise."

Okay, she could handle riding the horse. She'd done it for years in her earlier life. It didn't obligate her to anything else. Of course not.

Yeah, keep telling yourself that.

In moments, Mason had Sassy saddled and ready to go, as well as his own mount, a large buckskin. Conscious of Mason's eyes on her, Kris took a deep breath, put her foot in a stirrup, and pulled herself up into the saddle in a smooth movement.

Yes!

She wanted to pump her fist.

Mason made a sound of approval. "Not bad."

She tugged the reins, turning Sassy so she faced the man who ignited such sexual hunger in her, and grinned at him. "Damn straight."

She watched him mount up with a lithe, fluid movement and urge his horse forward.

"All set?"

Kris nodded. "After you."

The ride across the rolling pastureland was exhilarating and refreshing. They began at an easy lope, embraced by the sunlight's warmth. The wind felt so good against her skin, the feel of the horse beneath her bringing back so many memories. For a moment, as she and the animal streaked across the landscape, she forgot Afghanistan, forgot broken relationships, forgot everything except this moment and the incredible freedom sweeping through her.

Then, ahead of her, Mason slowed down and pulled his mount to a walk. She rode up alongside him.

"Why are we stopping?"

He pointed off to the left to a dense stand of ancient oak trees. "Thought we'd take a minute to enjoy nature. That's a pretty sight, and there's a creek where we can water the horses."

Dismount? Out here in the middle of nowhere? With him? Was he nuts? Was she?

Kris figured she definitely was because she nodded and urged Sassy to follow him to the spot he'd indicated. It really was beautiful. A narrow creek cut through the meadow here, the spot shaded by the heavy limbs of the very old trees. They dismounted and led their horses to the stream, standing quietly while the animals drank. The silence wrapped around them like a thick blanket, so Kris dug desperately around in her brain for some kind of conversation.

Mason touched her shoulder. "Let's make sure the horses don't decide to head home without us."

He took Sassy's reins and led both horses to one

of the trees where he looped the strips of leather over low-hanging branches.

Kris frowned. "Are we staying here for some reason?"

"We are." He walked back over to where she was standing.

"And that reason would be?" But she was sure she knew the answer before he said anything.

"This."

He grabbed her by the shoulders and pulled her roughly to his body, pressing her against him tightly enough she could feel the hard length of his cock through the fabric of his jeans. She closed her eyes, giving herself over to the sensations rioting through her. His mouth was like a hot branding iron on hers, searing her lips, his tongue probing and searching, forcing her to open for him so he could dive inside.

Walk away, she told herself. Push him away. Get back on the horse and get the hell out of here. This man is more than a client, he's big trouble. He pushed buttons she usually kept frozen in place. She was stupid to even have gone on this ride with him. She knew now what men meant when they said they were led around by their cocks. Being near Mason made her pussy clench and throb and her juices flow.

And her brain, obviously, take a vacation.

Completely unable to resist, she welcomed the intrusion of his tongue and let her own participate in the erotic dance.

His stroked up and down her back, the touch of his hands searing her even through the T-shirt she wore. Nerve endings crackled to life, sparking little explosions everywhere in her body. Her blood pumped in her veins, and her heart rate ratcheted up, the way it had been that night a year ago. The night she melted into him, her body craving his and everything she knew he could do to her. With her.

He lifted his head a fraction, and she opened her eyes to find his staring directly into hers.

"I'll give you one chance to tell me to stop. Just one. I keep remembering how great the sex between us was. Don't try to tell me you don't think the same thing. If you don't want this, I'll keep away from you the rest of the time you're here. Otherwise...."

He let the words trail off, his meaning clear. Unless she said no, he planned for them to have sex again while she was still here. And exactly how would that work?

"My team—" she began.

"You're smart. So am I. We'll figure it out." He

brushed his mouth over hers. "I'm not asking you for any kind of commitment here."

"Good." *Asshole.* "Because I don't plan to give one. I like my life plenty fine the way it is."

His muscles tensed. "So do I. Been there, done that, not willing to try it again." He paused. "But nothing says we can't enjoy each other when the opportunity presents itself. Not when the sex is off the charts."

He was certainly right about that. And good sex was certainly hard to find. She could attest to that. Still. She opened her mouth to say no, but instead what came out was, "All right."

He nipped her bottom lip. "Don't move."

She watched as he took something from behind his saddle and unrolled what appeared to be a blanket.

"You came prepared," she observed, not sure whether to be irritated or glad.

His smile was purely sexual. "I was hopeful."

Mason reached out his hand, she took it, and his mouth came down on hers again. The fire ignited. She was as hungry as he was, tasting him, dueling with his tongue. She reached up and anchored her fingers in his hair, holding his head in place. Mason reached down and tugged her T-shirt out of her jeans, sliding his hand beneath the fabric along her rib cage to cup a breast. The hot touch of his fingers grazed her through the thin satin of her bra.

She moaned when he pinched one nipple between thumb and forefinger and tugged gently. As he worked the hard bud, his mouth slid across her cheek to the line of her jaw. He sprinkled a light trail of kisses until he reached the spot behind her ear he knew drove her crazy and applied the tip of his tongue to it. Sensation splashed through her directly to her cunt, tremors vibrating in her internal muscles. Her panties were instantly soaked, the scent of her own musk drifting up to her nostrils. It mixed with the earthy aroma of Mason—something woodsy, a hint of horseflesh, and all male. She wanted to lick him all over, taste every inch of him as she'd done in that hotel room with the soft light of a lamp bathing them in its glow. At last, she could see all of him in the bright light of day. Her mouth watered at the prospect.

The slide of Mason's hot, wet mouth down the line of her neck was so erotic, she cried out in protest when he lifted his head. But, then, in seconds, he had her T-shirt and bra gone, tossed to the quilt, and that same searing mouth closed over one nipple while his fingers pinched and squeezed the other. Her legs were so shaky she could barely stand, digging her fingers into his hard biceps for balance.

He read her signals, lowering her to the quilt without moving either his mouth or his hand. She slipped her hands between them and began yanking on his shirt, pulling it from his jeans and digging for the buckle on his belt. She had gone from zero to one hundred on the ready meter from nothing more than his kisses and his touch. But hadn't he been able to do that to her the last time, too? And more than once. Many times more.

He lifted his head, giving the nipple one last lick.

"Not yet." He moved her hand from his waist. "If they come off now so will my self-control." His voice was rough with lust, the timbre of it reverberating through her. "There are things I want to do with you first. To you."

He disposed of her boots and slid her jeans down her legs, tossing them on top of her T-shirt. Kneeling between her thighs, he leaned down and took the lacy top edge of her panties in his teeth, slowly dragging them down the surface of her mound. When he had them barely past the tops of her thighs, he dipped his head and stroked his tongue along her slit, pushing the silky fabric into her drenched folds.

She fisted her hands in his hair, pulling him even closer, lifting herself to his teasing, clever touch. The pulse in her womb escalated, the beat vibrating through her body. She heard soft moaning and realized it was coming from her, as she thrust herself against his mouth. But overlaid was a growl rumbling from Mason's throat as he dragged her panties down farther and pressed his tongue against her clit.

When he finally pulled the scrap of satin the rest of the way down her body, she opened her legs for him, and his mouth closed over her. He licked her slit, probed her opening with his tongue, and swirled the tip around her sensitive clit. Sharp sensations rippled through her, from her pussy to her breasts to her painfully turgid nipples.

"More," she whimpered. "Inside me. I want you inside me."

He gave a rough laugh, the sound pulsating through her overstimulated cunt. "Not yet. I'm not through tasting you."

In the next instant, he thrust his stiffened tongue inside her, scraping it against her delicate walls. When he curled it enough to rasp the tip against her sweet spot, she was so primed in such a short time that she convulsed immediately, an orgasm washing over her. Her body shook and trembled, and she anchored herself with her hold on his hair. It was impossible to squeeze her legs together against the spasms, his broad shoulders holding them apart as he feasted and tasted and teased.

When the ripples subsided, at last, she unclenched her fingers from Mason's hair and let her arms fall to the side, her breathing a stutter in her throat. He lifted his eyes that had darkened to the color of espresso. His mouth glistened with the liquid from her pussy. Very slowly, he swiped his tongue across his bottom lip, the sight so erotic, her depleted body was instantly aroused again.

God! The man was going to kill her.

She grabbed the bottom of his shirt again and tugged it upward. Her hands itched to touch the hard planes of his chest and feel the softness of the dusting of hair covering it.

"Off," she urged. "Now. Please."

Mason's cock was hard as a spike, and he was so aroused he was afraid it would break through his jeans and his balls would explode. He had entertained the false hope that once he got his hands on Kris Gauthier again, it would satisfy the intense craving he'd been harboring for a year and that would be that, But the gods were having a huge laugh at his expense. Not only was his craving not appeased, it had ramped up to an unbelievable level.

She tasted as sweet as she had all those months ago, her scent as intoxicating. Maybe more. He was stunned by the thought he might never get enough of this woman, and then where would he be? This couldn't go anywhere except where it was right this moment. The disastrous destruction of his engagement had left him bitter about relationships. So what if he grew old alone. It was better than opening himself up to pain again.

Deliberately, he closed his mind to that train of thought. He had the hottest woman he'd ever met naked before him. He didn't plan to waste this moment being depressed about something he couldn't change, something that had happened more than a year ago.

He yanked his shirt over his head and tossed it to the side, bending low again to pepper soft kisses on her throat, both breasts, down the little swell of her tummy, to the soft curls on her mound. He paused a moment to inhale her scent, savoring the richness of it before pushing himself to his feet.

He toed off his boots and socks, disposed of his jeans and boxer briefs with one shove of his hands, and stood before her naked, one hand wrapped around his aching shaft. He was torn between wanting to jack off all over her soft, scented skin; have her lips wrapped around him; or slide home into her pussy and fucking her brains out.

Finally, knowing his control was hanging by a thread, he reached down to his jeans and dug a condom out of a pocket.

Kris's eyes widened. "Do you always carry one of those around with you?"

"No, only when I have something planned." He let his gaze rake the length of her body. "And I've definitely been planning this since I laid eyes on you again."

His hands actually trembled as he rolled the latex on his swollen cock and knelt again between her thighs. Spreading the lips of her pussy wide, he nudged at her with his dick, prodding her opening. He entered her slowly, savoring every hot inch of his entry. When he was fully seated inside her, he reached beneath her and palmed the cheeks of her ass, his fingers finding the hot crease.

"Remember when I fucked you here?" He barely recognized the hoarse voice as his own.

"Yes." The word came out on a whisper of a sigh. Her eyes blazed at the memory, darkening to the blue of a stormy ocean.

"Before you leave the Double R, I'm going to do it again. I want you to suck my cock again, play with my balls while I shove my tongue onto your sweet cunt. And when we can't last another minute, I'm going to turn you over, lube up that sweet, hot tunnel, and fill you so full of me, you'll explode."

Her small pink tongue came out to wet her lips, a habit that only made him harder.

"Would you like that?" He pressed into her again.

"Yessss," she hissed. "Yes, yes, yes."

Her fingers dug into his biceps as he moved over her. "Then count on it."

He couldn't wait one moment more. Lifting her to him, fingers digging into that hot crevice, he pounded into her, hitting the mouth of her womb with every stroke. She cried out but met him thrust for thrust. Soon there was nothing but the two of them, a cloud of heat scorching them, his thick shaft in her tight wet pussy, and the sexual tension building in his body.

He watched her, remembering from their first time together what the signals were, and when she was close to the peak, he ramped up his movement, hips pistoning. They exploded together, a cataclysmic eruption that shook them both. He held her tight to his body, the walls of her cunt squeezing his cock as it pulsed over and over again.

He lost track of time, had no idea how many seconds or minutes the climax lasted. Finally, though, the aftershocks lessened then subsided. He managed to drag enough air into his lungs to catch his breath, and his heart rate slowed to a manageable rhythm. He rolled to the side, taking Kris with him, unwilling to break their connection yet. Their sweat-slicked bodies were glued together, and he relished every point of contact.

When his dick began to soften, he eased himself from her wet clasp, carefully removed the condom, stuffed it into the foil packet, and turned to her again. Impulsively, he pressed a kiss to her lips, a soft one, not erotic, but full of so much tenderness, it shocked him.

He saw by the look in her eyes it stunned her,

also.

"Mason?"

A question, and the sound of it so intimate it made something in his heart turn over. Exactly what was she asking? Nothing he wanted to answer. Not now. Not ever. He was prepared for hot, raunchy sex and nothing more. Nada. Zip. And certainly not with a woman who irritated the crap out of him.

And why is that, jerkhead? Because you're afraid you feel something else for her? Afraid she'd laugh at you if you said something?

He was never going down that road again. Easing her from his arms, he rose and walked, naked, back to his horse. From one of the saddlebags, he grabbed two towels he'd tossed in at the barn and threw one to her.

"We'd better get back before people start asking questions."

She shuttered her eyes, any emotion reflected in them disappearing. Good. Better for both of them. Sex, he reminded himself. Plain, raunchy sex.

He took the towel from her, when she'd finished wiping the perspiration from her body, and handed her the clothes she'd been wearing. Then he deliberately turned around to dress himself, the movement a symbolic closing of a door. When they were both ready, he rolled up the quilt and tied it behind the saddle again, stowed the towels, and freed the horses.

When he handed Kris the reins to Sassy, she stared at him for what seemed an eternity, her expression unreadable. Then, as smoothly as she'd done earlier, she swung up into the saddle and settled herself. Mason mounted his own horse and urged him forward, nodding for Kris to follow.

The ride back seemed both endless and too short. He wanted it to be over, yet he didn't want it to end. Halfway there, Kris urged her horse into a canter and let the mare run full out, only slowing when they got closer and she needed to let the animal cool down. Mason lagged behind in a slower canter, admiring the way she sat a horse and the effortless control she had. A perfect match for a ranch.

Someone else's, he reminded himself sternly. Not mine. Never mine.

But he'd have her again, before she and her team left. He'd make sure to imprint his presence on her without interfering with her job, and then one more night of down-and-dirty sex. He was sure that would get her out of his system, once and for all.

Chapter Four

Everyone was already digging into breakfast when Kris made it into the ranch house the next morning. She'd hoped by this time Mason would have eaten and gone to do whatever it was he normally did during the day.

Yesterday, as soon as she'd cooled her horse down and put her tack away, she'd disappeared into the bunkhouse. Last night, she'd had Lane ask Martina to fix a plate he could bring down to the bunkhouse for her. Her excuse was she wanted to spend more time studying the maps and going over some reports.

Avoiding Mason was more like it.

It was painfully obvious to her their sexual chemistry was so strong that just being with him zinged her brain waves. Having him fly in the copilot's seat with her had been a big mistake, but she was torn between keeping miles of distance between them and treating him as she would any other client.

Why hadn't she been smart and called Grey when she'd discovered who they were working for. She could have asked for reassignment?

Because you don't want him to see you as different than the other agents, different than the men who work for him.

And every time she gave in to her desire for sex with Mason, she was digging a deeper hole for herself.

Damn it all, anyway.

This morning, she had no excuse to avoid breakfast up at the house. She just made up her mind to ignore him and get on with business. She had some flying she wanted to do today and some information to go over with the team. She'd make herself plenty busy.

Her team was already seated and serving themselves.

"So, last night, we got nada." Lane scooped scrambled eggs onto his plate and added some strips of bacon. "A couple of times, I got a blip from one of the sensors, but the heat signature wasn't big enough for a human. Not even a small one."

"Lots of wild animals out there," Mason told him, reaching for the large basket of biscuits. "Raccoons, foxes, coyotes. Whole bunch of different ones."

"Yeah." Ted nodded. "We've had that before, animals tripping the sensors. We learned the hard way how to tell the difference."

"This isn't our first time in the wilds of Texas." Kris hadn't meant to snap the words, but apparently she had, because Lane gave her a puzzled look. She cleared her throat. "I meant we've been in terrain like this before."

"We get it." Mason's voice was uninflected, the expression on his face unreadable.

Kris took an empty seat on the other side of the table, as far away from Mason as she could get. This was not going to be easy, when being in the same room with him sent her temperature into the red zone and her body humming with need. Maybe this was a disease, and she could find a cure. If not, she was in big trouble.

Yesterday could not happen again. No matter how much she wanted it. She was a freaking leader of a high-security ops team, for heaven's sake. She could remain motionless watching for bad guys for hours, fly circles around nearly every other chopper pilot, and outscore every member of her team on the range. Except Ted, with his rifle, if course. Surely, she could keep her hormones in check for a few days.

Ray filled his own plate then shifted his gaze to Mason. "Ted and I thought we'd take a ride out to the area again today, if it's okay with you."

"We mapped it and entered the coordinates last time," Ted added, "so we don't need to borrow Stick again."

"I don't mind." Stick grinned. "Beats chasing cows all day."

Mason glanced at hm. "Ha ha. Very funny. Ted, if you need him, he's all yours."

"We're good."

Mason narrowed his eyes. "It's easy to get lost out there."

"We've been in harder places to get around," she snapped. Then took a breath. "Sorry. But by this time I bet we could do this with our eyes closed. You do stuff like this often enough, you learn how to absorb info really fast."

He lifted his hands. "Sorry. No offense here."

"None taken." She focused on the food on her plate.

What the hell was wrong with her? She could certainly be civil to the man. He'd given her the best sex she'd ever had in her life, for damn sure. If she said she hadn't enjoyed, it she'd be lying. It wasn't as if she wanted anything else from him, right? And maybe, if she was lucky and didn't act like someone on a hormone binge, she might get to have some again before this gig was over.

Steady, she told herself. Calm. And businesslike. Be your usual self.

Except, at the moment, she wasn't sure who her usual self was. The hardened military veteran, the pilot who'd flown so many SOAR missions? The experienced team leader from The Omega Team? Or maybe the woman who'd been hiding behind both of them for too many years?

Don't overthink it, and don't piss him off. He's a client. And what harm would one more session of scorching sex do, anyway?

She saw him watching her, his face expressionless. But the heat and sizzle was still there in his eyes. Oh, yeah. It was definitely there.

"You sure?" Stick asked.

"Sure?" She frowned. She'd already lost the thread of the conversation. Shit. What she needed to do was put Mason and hot sex out of her mind until they had everything together here. Compartmentalize, as she'd been able to do for years. If only she could get yesterday out of her mind. "Sure about what?"

"That they don't need me." Stick chuckled.

"Having trouble keeping up this morning, boss?" Lane joked.

Kris ignored him, concentrating instead on seasoning her eggs and buttering her biscuit. She swallowed a mouthful of food before she spoke, certain she had herself back under control.

"I'm going to fly over the area one more time." She smiled at Martina as the woman filled her coffee mug. "I know we took a ton of still shots and video, but I want to get some of where the Double R borders the ranches on either side and also follow the path of the Rio Grande where it borders the edge of the land."

"Need me to come with?" Mason threw the question out there, almost offhanded, but she heard the little edge in his tone. What did that mean? Did he want to fly with her or not?

She gave him a polite smile. "I think we've got it. You must have work to do."

"Actually, they finished the branding yesterday. If you don't need Stick, he and Greg will keep things together." His mouth curved in that slightly sardonic grin she was coming to know. "Besides, I like watching you fly that thing."

God! He was such a chameleon—uptight and

remote one minute then friendly the next. Okay, she'd put on her team-leader personality and act like he was any other male client in the world. She could do that. She'd flown missions where she nearly got killed. Surely she could handle one hot rancher.

"Fine." She glanced down at her watch. "Meet me in the field in an hour. That will give Ted and Ray time to get headed into the area we're watching and me time to plot exactly what I want to see."

He nodded. "I'll be there."

Her gaze tracked him as he strode from the room, long legs encased in worn jeans, the muscles in his ass flexing so nicely, back straight, shoulders broad. Okay, so maybe one more night, and she'd get him out of her system. At least, that was her plan.

*****

They were in Mateo's living room. Rigo sat in a straight-back chair across from his brother, who lounged on the couch, smoking a cigarillo.

"So, Rigo, you tell me you don't want to make another crossing right now."

Rigo swallowed and tightened his hands on the arms of the chair. "I'm saying that I think it would be unwise to do it so close to the other one. I don't want to have to kill anyone again."

"Pah." Mateo waved his hand. "Did we ever hear anything about the dead bodies? Did they post armed guards? Did you have trouble crossing the other night?"

"No. No, I did not." He shifted uncomfortably in his chair. "But that doesn't mean they won't be waiting the next time. I think we got lucky this time. Perhaps they haven't had a chance to prepare for us."

"Rigo, Rigo, Rigo." Mateo sighed, took a puff of his cigarillo, and blew a stream, of smoke into the air. "You worry needlessly. The Americano who owns that ranch is oblivious to all of this."

"Then why did he send two of his rancheros out to patrol that area? Men we were forced to kill?"

"My personal opinion? They've been dealing with poachers and cattle rustlers. If you hadn't cut the wrong fence that time, they'd never even think anything was happening there. Blame your own stupidity."

Rigo wanted to throw his hands up. How was it his brother could be smart enough to run this small offshoot of the Sinaloa Cartel so efficiently and lucratively, yet not see things right in front of his face.

"There can't be any poaching, Mateo." He blew out a sigh of exasperation. "There is not valuable wild game there, and that area of the ranch is so unsuitable for cattle, they never use it. That's one of the reasons we targeted it for our route."

A long moment of silence. Another pull on the cigarillo. Another stream of smoke.

Rigo waited impatiently.

"Here's the situation, little brother." Mateo uncrossed and recrossed his legs. "Our buyer wants a delivery tomorrow night. No wiggle room. He has distributors waiting. If he doesn't get it from us, he'll go elsewhere. We cannot afford that."

"But—"

Mateo held up his hand. "I have worked my fucking ass off to build this organization. It may be small, but it commands respect, and it commands authority. I get a seat at the Sinaloa table."

And that, Mateo thought, was the heart of the matter.

"I understand," he said slowly.

"Good." Mateo snapped the word out. "Then you know that tomorrow night happens without question. You have a group waiting, right? Then make your arrangements."

Rigo stared at his brother, saying nothing.

"I will send people with you." Mateo flicked his ash into a glass dish. "Two armed guards."

"So we can kill more people?" Rigo shook his head in exasperation. "That's not the solution."

"Take care of it. If you make a mess, I'll clean it up, but you will make the delivery."

"Exactly how will you clean it up?" A finger of unease tickled Rigo's back.

"You don't need to know. Do your job and everything will be fine. We'll use two vans tomorrow night. I will have two men meet you where you pick up the group. They'll have the merchandise with them, ready for transport. That's all."

Rigo knew when he'd been dismissed. As he left his brother's house, he pulled out his cell phone to call the man who assisted him with the crossings.

"We're on for tomorrow night. No," he replied, "I could not talk him out of it. You know Mateo when he digs in. He wants the glory at the Sinaloa table." He listened for a moment. "I know, I know. But we have no choice. So, gather the next ten and meet me at the warehouse." He started to hang up then remembered Mateo's final words. "We will have armed escorts. Not my choice. And they'll have another van. Let us pray no more lives need to be taken."

He shoved the phone back in his pocket and wondered if there was any place he could disappear that Mateo and the cartel could not find him.

*****

As the chopper lifted smoothly into the air, Mason again admired the efficiency and cool poise with which Kris handled the bird. She was all business, focused on managing the flight and controlling the sleek machine. He loved to watch the smooth play of muscles in her arms as she worked the controls and the deftness of her touch.

Her face was impossible to read, shielded as it was by her aviator shades and the bill of her ball cap. But nothing in the movements of her body or her posture betrayed the slightest degree of tension. It seemed, once she sat in the pilot's seat, she blocked everything else from her mind. A skill he was sure she'd learned before being accepted as a Nightstalker.

Below him, he could see Ray and Ted cantering across one of the fenced pasture sections. He was pleased to note that a wrangler had directed them around the areas with cattle to those acres that were empty. Soon, they were beyond the arable land and into the wild of the landscape, where they slowed their horses to a careful walk.

A crackle in his headset startled him and, in a moment, he heard Ted's voice.

"Ray and I want to ride the entirety of the unused acres today. We'll check the sensors first and then branch out. Any objections?"

"You're good to go." Kris's voice was clear and authoritative. "Report on the condition of the sensors, first."

"Will do."

Mason pressed the button that allowed him to switch to a channel only he and Kris could hear. He touched her arm to indicate what he was doing, and she nodded. Tapped her own switch on the flight controls.

"What are they trying to find?" he wanted to know.

"Signs that there has been traffic in other spots down there."

Mason frowned. "I thought they checked it yesterday."

"They did, but after studying all the shots we took, I'm assuming they want to eyeball it close up.

Something they saw must have triggered it."

"You think they'd cross my land in more than one place? What about that dirt road we saw out to the highway?"

She shrugged, a graceful lift of her shoulders. "That's the most likely scenario, but we never leave anything to chance. It can get you killed." She banked the helo into a turn. "Okay, I'm going to fly a zigzag pattern, from your neighbor on one side to the one on the other, covering every bit of the empty land down there."

"For what purpose?"

"Possible alternate routes. Avenues they might choose if they decide for some reason yours is too risky. Although you certainly have the ideal spot for them."

"Yeah, lucky me."

But after more than an hour, she finally called it quits.

"Heading back," she radioed to the men below. "See you when you get in with a full report."

"Roger that," Ray answered.

"So nothing?" Mason asked.

"The ranches on either side of you use every bit of their land, right down to the river. I'm guessing that if the coyotes tried to bring people through, they'd have trouble with the cattle and create a disturbance."

"You got that right."

"Plus, I didn't see any other egress to the highway without going past either ranch house. So, your ranch is definitely the prime target." She pointed at the ground. "What's that? That cabin at the edge of one section."

"It used to be an old line shack. A few years ago, I refurbished it, added water and electricity. Bought some new furniture."

"Any special reason?"

Yes. I planned to bring my fiancée there for a romantic getaway on the ranch. Until she decided there was room in her bed for men besides me.

"One that no longer exists." He hadn't meant to spit the words out with such bitterness.

Kris gave a quick turn of her head to catch his expression before staring out the windshield again. "Okay. Sounds like it might be a nice place, though."

"Not close enough for whoever is crossing my land to make use of," he pointed out. "Too far away from the unused acres."

"Yeah, I figured. Eyeballing it from here I could

see that. But I was curious, anyway."

"How long do you think we'll have to wait before they try another crossing?"

"Hard to say. Under normal circumstances, I'd say not for another week or so."

"Shit." He spat the word. "So, we, what, sit around waiting?"

"Part of the job," she reminded him. "We do a lot of waiting. But I said, under normal circumstances. I have an itch between my shoulder blades that tells me they might be pushing that date up."

"What makes you think that?"

"Experience. Instincts. Whatever." She turned the chopper toward the ranch. "I'm going to call Grey when I get back and see if he'd got any data for me that relates to this situation. That's in addition to whoever we have on the streets. We have people in the office who monitor texts and conversations and anything else that goes out in cyberspace. He's had people checking out the chatter in the drug pipelines, and he may have picked something up for us."

"Let's hope."

As soon as Kris landed the chopper and completed her shutdown, she fished out her cell phone and speed dialed a number.

"Grey? Yeah, we're still checking. Got anything for me from the gossip line? Yeah? Okay, I'll put you on speaker so the client can hear, too."

"You there, Mason?" Grey's gravelly voice came through with a surprising minimum of static.

"I am."

"Okay. Glad Kris put us on speaker. Saves her having to repeat it."

"So, what have you got?" Mason asked.

"I'll spare you all the who said whats. We've been doing a lot of digging here and monitoring what we call the smuggling gossip line."

Mason couldn't help grinning. "Do I even want to know how you do that?"

"Not at all. But you should be aware that there's chatter the group using your spread is a small group that broke off from the Sinaloa cartel."

"Drugs." Mason's stomach clenched. "Kris said you suspected that."

"We did," Grey agreed. "If it was a coyote hauling a group of illegals and nothing more, they wouldn't have bothered to shoot your men. The coyote would have beat feet and left the poor saps to whatever authorities you called."

"What else?" Kris asked. "If Sinaloa's involved in

this, we might need to expand the team."

"Like I said," Grey answered. "This group is a small offshoot. A baby cartel on its own, you might say. But their leader has a seat at the Sinaloa table, and he's not going to want to lose face."

"I thought they might stop after they killed my men," Mason told him.

"This guy has buyers waiting. He's probably using the illegals as mules, and he'll want to make the deliveries on time. Your sheriff isn't equipped to deal with them, and the Border Patrol is way undermanned. The dealers know this and take full advantage."

"Damn arrogant of them."

Grey's short laugh held no humor. "No shit. I'm sure Kris told you their schedule is erratic, deliberately so, and they don't make the treks too close together. But, because they had to kill two of your men, they'd wait to see what you were going to do. They might not make a trip across your property for a week or maybe two. But we've picked up conversations about a deal going down either tonight or tomorrow night. Seems the buyer is putting pressure on, and the boss wants a victory before a big cartel leader meet next week."

"We'll be ready," Kris assured him.

"I can add my men to the mix," Mason put in.

"Not necessary," Grey told him. "This team is trained for this. And we don't want any more of your hands getting in the way of a drug dealer's bullet."

Mason had to agree. "Fine. But we're here for anything the team needs."

"And thanks for that." The man laughed. "Understand you've been feeding them real well. Setting up some stiff competition for other assignments."

"We aim to please."

"Okay, boss. We'll be ready. Thanks for the update." She disconnected the call and stuck the cell phone back in her jeans pocket. "I'm going to call Ted and Ray back in. They'll need to get some sleep this afternoon if we're going to pull an all-nighter. Same for me."

"You'll be out there with them?"

Kris shook her head. "No, I'll be in the bunkhouse with Lane, monitoring the sensors. The others will be out there, concealed and armed. But I have to be ready to move the minute they need me." She opened the door on her side of the cockpit. "Let me get my men in and then, if Martina can throw a quick lunch together, I'll get them back to the bunkhouse."

"We'll take care of it."

She turned in her seat, her hand on the door, and pulled down her sunglasses to the bridge of her nose. As much as she might think she was hiding it, there was no mistaking either the heat or the hunger in her eyes. She opened her mouth as if she was about to say something. Mason tried to wait patiently, but she shook her head, pushed the door wide open, and jumped down to the ground.

Okay, so timing was working against them. But he'd have her again before this was over. She wanted it, too, no matter how much she might try to hide it. He'd have to figure out a way to make it happen.

*****

Kris was ready to scream. It seemed, every time she turned around, Mason was right there. Next to her. Near her. Asking her if she needed anything. She half expected him to sit and watch her while she slept in the bunkhouse, but he'd had enough sense not to do that.

Still, since yesterday, while they'd planned and

rested and waited, he had been a constant presence. She wondered if her team would start asking questions. No, he was the client. And former military. They'd expect him to be involved. And be everywhere they were.

The night had passed without incident. The feedback from a couple of the sensors was, again, caused by some of the abundant wildlife wandering in that sector. The men returned to the ranch, ate breakfast, and rolled into their bunks. Even Mason had headed up to the house to catch a few hours of shut-eye. Tonight, they'd all be at it again.

She finally crawled up into her own bunk and dropped into a dead sleep. The touch of a hand on her shoulder woke her. Reflex took over, and she sat up, gun in hand, pointed at whoever was touching her.

"Hey, hey, hey." Lane grinned and backed away, hands up. "It's me. Don't shoot."

"Sorry." She rubbed her hand over her face. "Old habits never go away."

"Nor should they. Anyway, we're going up to the house for lunch, and the client is on the porch, waiting to have a few words with you."

She frowned. "About what?"

"Not my department, but he's got a cooler with him. Maybe he wants a private lunch and powwow."

"It's business, nothing more." She hated that she sounded so defensive.

"Makes no never mind to me. You call the shots. You're the leader." He started toward the door then turned back. "And, by the way, a damn fine one."

Then, he was out the door. Kris took a few minutes to use the bathroom, wash her face, and brush her hair into a better ponytail. Hauling in a deep breath, she went out to meet Mason. And, yes, Lane was right. The man was holding a medium-size cooler.

She glanced from him to the cooler and back again. "Are we taking a trip?"

"A short one. If you're okay with that." He waved in the direction of the house. "Your team is eating lunch and then going over the plans, again. I figured you could take a short time out."

Her breath caught in her throat. She knew damn well what was behind this sudden picnic. "You did, huh?"

He motioned behind him, where a bright red ATV sat. "I figured that would be faster than horses. Come on. I'll give you an up-close look at that cabin."

Her gaze met his. They both knew, if she got onto that ATV, exactly what would happen. Okay. They might not have anything beyond this moment in time, nor should they, but damn it, she might as well enjoy it.

Still, she made a last-ditch effort. "I don't think this is such a good idea."

He cupped her chin and tilted her face up to his. "You afraid of me, Kris? Afraid to be with me?"

"Hell, no." She jerked her head away. "It's just sex, anyway. Right?"

So many seconds ticked by as he studied her face, she wanted to smack him.

"Well?" she prompted. "We don't even like each other."

"That remains to be seen. Come on. Let's give it a shot."

She took his hand, the heat flaming through her bloodstream.

Big mistake, Krissy girl. Big, big mistake.

*****

They lay side by side on the bed in the cabin, clothes tossed aside on the nearby chair, bodies slick with sweat. Lunch had been filled with small talk and casual touches. No wine, no alcohol of any kind because they would need to be at their sharpest for the evening. But that hadn't affected the intensity of their passion. The sex had been hot, intense, and erotic.

Mason stroked his fingers down her cheek. "I figured this might help get you out of my system, but who am I kidding? I don't know if that will ever happen. And I'm not sure what to do about it."

She turned so she lay facing him. "I feel the same way. It's a bitch, isn't it? You know this doesn't change anything between us, right?"

"No kidding." He rolled her on top of him and threaded his fingers through her hair, holding her head in place. "I have no idea how you see the rest of your life, but I'm a really bad bet, Kris."

"Is that so? Tell me exactly how."

He tore his gaze away from hers. "I've been a lone wolf all my life. Never even wanted to settle with someone, share my life with them."

"You did once," she reminded him.

His grip on her tightened. "Taught me a lesson, too."

"Mason, all women aren't like your former

almost-fiancée."

He shifted his gaze back to her face. "What about you? You've carved out a life for yourself. Where would you fit any man into your schedule with The Omega Team?"

She hesitated. Emotions he couldn't identify, or maybe didn't want to, flashed across her face.

"You're right," she said at last. "This is all we should focus on. Maybe sometime—" She bit off her words. "Forget it."

Before he could ask what she meant, she licked his lips with the tip of her tongue, teasing him until he opened for her. She swept inside, and he moved his own tongue to duel and dance with hers. God, he loved her taste, everywhere on her body. He could get drunk on it, he was sure.

He rubbed his hands up and down the slope of her back and the sweet curve of her ass. His fingers crept into the hot crease there, pressing against the tiny opening.

"Today," he told her, tearing his mouth away from hers, "I'm going to fuck you in your ass so hard you'll remember it well after you're gone. And give you an orgasm that will blow the top of your head off. You'll dream about this, Kris. Think about this every night."

That odd look came into her eyes again, a brief flash before it was gone.

"Okay. I want that, too. I'm tired of fighting it. We need to do this and get it out of our systems."

"Then get ready for a hard ride."

In seconds, he had shifted her aside, rolled on a condom, and lifted her over him. Very slowly, he lowered her onto his dick, which seemed to be perpetually hard when he was around her, no matter the amount of sex they'd already had.

She slid onto him easily, still so wet and ready for him, it took his breath away. The tight walls of her pussy clamped around him, gripping him like a wet fist.

"Slow and easy," he ground out between clenched teeth. "I want to make it last."

"Me, too," she told him in a breathless voice.

And that's exactly what it was. She rode him like a wild thing, breasts bouncing, head thrown back, hair flying. He gripped her hips hard, guiding her, stabilizing her, holding himself back once he felt the first tremors begin in her cunt. It took every ounce of discipline but somehow he managed.

When the tremors finally subsided, he lifted her

from his body and placed her beside him on her hands and knees. Her body still trembled, so he shoved pillows beneath her to steady her. He reached for the tube of gel he'd placed on the little table next to the bed, squeezed a generous amount onto a finger, and slowly began to massage it into her rectum.

Jesus, she was hot there. Her tissues squeezed the hell out of him, as he probed and massaged. He added a second finger, stretching and scissoring to get her ready for him. Her choppy breathing rasped in the air, and she rocked back against his touch. Moans drifted from her and filled the air with the sound of sexual need.

"Ready?" He barely recognized the rough voice as his own.

"Yes, please. Now."

He sheathed himself, pressed the head of his cock against her opening, and carefully eased himself inside.

Jesus! The sensation was as hot as he remembered.

"Play with yourself," he ground out. "Touch your clit. Do it."

When she moved one arm to slide a hand

between her thighs, the movement tilted her ass in the air and pushed harder against his intrusion. Mason gritted his teeth, took a deep breath, and began a steady, in-and-out thrust. He tried to take it slow, but his balls ached, and his cock swelled even more.

"Almost there." He barely got the words out. "Ready?"

She nodded, her hips moving in cadence with his.

They exploded together, a soul-shattering climax that ripped apart every shred of their joined bodies. They shuddered together, gripped in an orgasm so powerful it robbed him of breath and nearly made his heart stop. On and on, the spasms went, shaking them with their intensity, until, at last, when he was sure he was about to pass out, they slowly subsided.

When he could breathe again, he eased from the clasp of her body, stripped off the condom, and rolled to his side. Hooking an arm around Kris's waist, he pulled her against him, unwilling to lose contact yet. Something had happened here today, between them, something in their frantic coupling he didn't want to examine. Or even admit.

Had she felt it, too?

They lay like that, locked together, for several moments before Kris pushed up and locked her gaze with his. He tried to read the message in hers, wondered what she saw in his. For a moment, he thought she was going to kiss him, but then she rolled away.

"Time to get back. We need to get ready to catch the bad guys."

With those words the mood was broken. Fine. That's what he wanted, too, right?

Absolutely.

"Let's get it done."

He rose and reached for his clothes. They dressed silently, not even acknowledging each other. Yeah, something had changed in a minute, something during that most intimate, most personal coupling. But Kris didn't appear to want to bring it up, so neither did he. Everything was better this way.

Kris pulled her hair back into its usual ponytail. "Time to get our act together."

Mason wondered if that would even be possible where Kris was concerned. Instead of solving his problem with a healthy dose of raunchy sex, all he'd done was create more need, a stronger hunger.

When she turned around, dressed, to face him,

he was shocked to see her face wiped of all expression. "Ready?"

"Absolutely." Ready to drag you back into bed.

And exactly how do you plan to handle that, asshole?

A question that riddled his mind as he locked the cabin, helped Kris onto the ATV, and cranked the engine. Too bad he didn't have any answers.

*****

They were all deployed tonight, every one of them. Mason had convinced Kris to include him, using his time in the military as a bonus, and she had grudgingly agreed. The air between them was tense, more so than it had been since the moment she'd set foot on his ranch. The vibes they gave off had to do with a lot more than sexual hunger, but he damn sure didn't want to dig into what it was.

Not tonight, for sure, when they all needed to block out everything except what was about to happen.

Kris flew everyone on the team—all six members—out to the last of the cleared pastures at dusk and parked the chopper behind a large copse of trees. While Lane waited in the chopper with the monitoring program on his computer, the rest dropped to the ground and took cover in the dense copse, waiting for word to move. Each of them was armed, and each had night vision goggles.

He was stunned to see Kris take up a position with them, a rifle cradled in her arms. When he opened his mouth to say something, she shook her head and touched her finger to her lips. She'd told him she'd be back at the bunkhouse monitoring the sensors with Lane. What had changed her mind? Of course, she had every right to be there as the leader of the team. And where had this protective shit come from, anyway? She could more than take care of herself.

This whole situation with Kris was driving him nuts. He wished he knew how she really felt. But, then, he'd have to examine his own feelings, and he didn't know if he was ready for that. Somewhere along the way "just sex" had morphed into something else. Something he didn't know if he was ready for. Or if Kris was.

Stop it, jackass. Concentrate on business.

Mason knew this had to be timed right to the second. If, indeed, the smugglers took a group across tonight, it was imperative to wait until they were all not only on the Texas side of the river, but also well onto Mason's property.

There was no moon tonight, a perfect cover for the smugglers, so they were completely dependent on the sensors to signal them. Time dragged, but he was used to it, as he was sure the others were, also. He had shifted his position slightly when he heard three clicks in his earbud.

The sensors had tripped.

Showtime!

Pulling down his NVGs, he moved stealthily, taking cover behind giant, thorny shrubs where he could. He could see the team members creeping along and, off to his right, the line of illegals. But instead of the one coyote leading them, he counted four people, three of them heavily armed, shepherding the group. Did the others see them?

Of course they did. These were seasoned veterans. He knew he needed to wait for Kris's signal to act.

It came only seconds later. Three clicks in his earbuds again.

"Everyone stop right where you are." Ray's voice boomed across the wasteland. In the next second, he turned on the flood he carried, bathing the shocked group in light.

"Drop your weapons," Ted ordered. "Everyone not armed come here to me, and you won't be hurt. The rest of you, drop your weapons."

Confusion exploded. The man at the head of the group turned to his guards, who shouldered their rifles. The illegals dropped to the ground, aware only that they needed to stay out of the way of any bullets. One of the guards fired toward the floodlight, shattering it, but the NVGs pierced the darkness, turning everything green.

Then the shooting began in earnest, bullets flying, people screaming. Mason took out one of the guards, someone else took out another one and, in seconds, it was all over. The coyote and the other guard put their hands behind their heads, ordered to their knees by Ray. Lane was out of the chopper and, in minutes, the coyote and the guards were flex-cuffed and the illegals herded away from the action where they huddled in panic.

"I called the sheriff." Kris was right at his shoulder. "He's sending vans to pick these people up and turn them over to Border Patrol, along with the nasties. We need to keep a lid on things for a few minutes, okay?"

"I don't think these people will stop," Lane said, approaching from the left, "but at least they won't be using your land anymore, Mason."

"Thank god for that."

"Hey, Kris?" Lane's voice, close to him, was underlined with concern. "What's that all over your shirt? You don't look so good. Jesus Christ! Mason, she's been shot."

"What? I...."

Mason turned in time to catch Kris in his arms as she collapsed. He kept on his NVGs so he could see better, and what he saw made him want to throw up. Her T-shirt was dark and wet, covered with what was obviously her blood. For one moment, his heart stopped then he moved into action. He ripped off her goggles and laid her on the ground, gently probing for the bullet wound.

"Damn!" He stared at Lane. "She was hit on the left, right below the shoulder. I don't know what's hit internally, but she's bleeding like a stuck pig. We need to get her out of here."

"I can fly the chopper," the man assured him. "I'm her backup."

"Then let's get the fuck out of here. Have the

other guys sit on everyone until the sheriff gets here. Let's roll."

Mason ripped off his own shirt to make a pressure bandage for Kris before lifting her in his arms. Holding her steady, he carried her as fast as he could to the helo.

"Where to?" Lane asked as the blades began their whine.

"County General. You can radio them. They've got a helipad. Come on. Move it."

The flight seemed endless, even though, in actuality, it took less than twenty minutes. The moment they hit the helipad, an emergency team ran to them with a gurney and whisked Kris away.

"Go with her," Lane shouted. "I'll go back with the helo and get the others. Catch." He tossed something to Mason. "Kris's cell. I'm speed dial one. Let us know what's what."

The chopper lifted off, and Mason ran for the entrance to the hospital.

*****

"You scared the shit out of me." Mason handed Kris a glass of wine then climbed back onto the bed next to her. "I nearly died myself in that hospital, waiting to find out if you were okay."

They were back in the cabin, where they'd spent a good deal of time since Kris had been discharged from the hospital three weeks before. Oh, he'd moved her directly into his room at the ranch, but here they could be completely alone. Have total privacy. They hadn't yet talked about what came next.

So far, she was still on medical leave from The Omega Team. Grey had flown out himself to check on her. On both of them. And told Kris not to hurry back to work.

She gave a soft laugh. "I didn't think you cared, big guy."

"Oh, I cared. Care." He was deadly serious. This was the first time they'd approached anything personal since he brought her home. He'd been giving her space and time to heal.

Questions were reflected in her eyes. "Do you? Really?"

"Bet your ass. I didn't realize how much until I thought I'd lost you." He ran his knuckle lightly down her cheek. "That night I was more frightened than

I've been in, oh, maybe, forever. I thought for sure I'd lost you. Even when they said you were okay, I wasn't sure I believed them."

She smiled. "I heard they had to bar the doors to Recovery to keep you out."

"Damn straight. That doctor told me the wound appeared worse than it was, that nothing vital had been hit. But I wanted to see for myself." He leaned on his elbow, resting his head on his palm. "That's when I realized what I really feel for you. It's about a lot more than the sex, Kris." He chuckled. "Although that's still off the charts."

"Or it would be, if you'd stop treating me like an invalid. The doctor has signed off on me, and I'm good as new. Or almost."

"Indulge me. Okay?" He paused, searching for the right words, not wanting to scare her away. "I never thought I'd feel this way about another woman. I think, at first, I resented you because you lit emotions inside me I thought I'd locked away."

She reached up and stroked his cheek. Wet her lower lip with her tongue. "Me, too, Mason. I had a lot of time to think while I was in the hospital. What happened that night reminded me how short life can really be. How it can be snatched away in a moment."

"Too true," he agreed.

She searched his face, obviously looking for something. Some kind of answer. "So tell me, big guy. What exactly do you feel?"

They'd grown so close, these last few weeks, their relationship taking twists and turns they'd never expected. But was she ready to hear this? He blew out a breath. It was now or never.

"I love you, Kris. I want you in my life, however we have to manage it."

She took so much time to respond, he felt disappointment bubble up inside him. Then she smiled.

"I love you, too, Mason. I want us to have a chance at this. I really do. We need to be careful because we both carry a lot of baggage but, I say, let's take the leap together."

"I'll do my best to deal with your job." He touched his mouth to hers briefly. "I'll worry, but I'll be here every time you come home."

Home. He liked the sound of that.

"Yeah, about that." She shifted slightly against him.

He tensed, wondering what monkey wrench was about to be thrown into the works. But he tried to be casual when he spoke.

"Lay it on me."

"While I was lying around, being a sloth, and you were out hustling your ass on the ranch, I did some research. Made some phone calls."

"About?" he prompted.

"Seems the medical chopper service that covers the area needs another pilot. They're very interested in talking to me, when I'm ready."

He widened his eyes in astonishment. "You'd leave The Omega Team? What about Grey and The Omega Team? Won't you miss the job?"

She shook her head. "Not at all. I think I've had all the adrenaline rush I can handle for a good while. And when Grey flew out to see me again last week, we had an extensive talk. He agrees it's time for me to make some changes."

"You'd be satisfied living on a ranch?" He gave her a hard stare. "Living with me?"

She wound her arms around his neck. "I couldn't think of anything I'd like more."

For the first time in years, pure happiness coursed through him, and the internal walls he'd built crumbled away.

"Then, get ready to be a rancher's wife, Miss

Gauthier." He winked. "Soon to be Mrs. Rowell."

She smiled back at him. "I'm ready. Let's get it done."

For a long time after that, no more words were spoken.

None were needed.

About the Author

Known as the oldest living author of erotic romance, Desiree Holt has produced more than two hundred titles in nearly every subgenre of romance fiction. Her stories are enriched by her personal experiences, her characters by the people she meets. After fifteen ears in the great state of Texas she relocated back to Florida to be closer to members of her family and a large collection of friends. Her favorite pastimes are watching football, reading, and researching her stories.

Learn more about her and read her novels here:

www.desireeholt.com

www.desiremeonly.com

www.facebook.com/desireeholtauthor

www.facebook.com/desireeholt

Twitter @desireeholt

Pinterest: desiree02holt

Google: www.desiree02holt

LinkedIn: www.LinkedIn.com/desiree01holt

Made in United States
Cleveland, OH
19 January 2025